Praise for *State of*

D0006032

A lively, diverse mystery with enjoya
and a relatable young female protagonist.

Kirkus Reviews

An impressively original, exceptionally well written,
thoroughly entertaining, and unreservedly recommended read
for children ages 7-12.
Midwest Book Review

Kitty Felde is teaching our children all about Capitol Hill in a
way that grabs and keeps their interest. Personally, I can say
she knows every nook and cranny of the place because she
interviewed me in almost all of them.
Former U.S. Senator Barbara Boxer

In an era of bitter partisan politics, it's a sneaky way to excite
the next generation about government and the possibility of
public service.

Former Chair of the House Armed Services Committee
Congressman Buck McKeon

"State of the Union" is a heartwarming read, a gem of a book.

Ginger Park, author of "The Hundred Choices
Department Store" and "The Royal Bee"

Another stellar entry in Kitty Felde's outstanding Fina
Mendoza Mystery series, "State of the Union" has it all – a
protagonist you will cheer for, warmth and humor, and a good
mystery story underpinning it all.
Jan Burke, author of the Irene Kelly Mysteries

Chesapeake Press
11111 Jefferson Blvd. Suite 3334, Culver City, CA 90231-3334
Visit us at: www.chesapeakepress.org

First Edition

Cover art courtesy of Imelda Hinojosa
The text for this book was set in Palatino Linotype

State of the Union/ Kitty Felde
ISBN 978-1-7359767-9-2 (paperback)
ISBN 978-1-7370978-1-5 (hardback)
LCCN 2021908034

For Oscar and Martha:
your immigration story still inspires me

ALSO BY KITTY FELDE:

Welcome to Washington Fina Mendoza

State of the Union

A Fina Mendoza Mystery

Kitty Felde

Chesapeake Press
Washington, DC

Chapter One

The basement was not my favorite place in the U.S. Capitol. It was dark and confusing and okay, I had to admit it, it was scary. There were twists and turns so you had to be careful not to crash into a congressman running for an elevator with a bottle of energy drink in his hand. I only did that once. Now, I was careful. Especially around the Capitol Carry Out.

The snack bar's real name was the Capitol Market, but everybody called it the Carry Out. Because that was what you did, you carried out your food.

That was what I was doing tonight, carrying a turkey sandwich for Papa and flaming hot chips, hot chocolate, and a banana for me. The guy in front of me at the register kept pointing his phone at the little machine to get the Bite app to work. The app was like electronic money, but the only thing you could buy with it was food at one of the Capitol snack bars. He kept trying and trying. I was having a hard time juggling my food. My banana slipped and landed on his foot. "Sorry," I said.

He turned and looked down at me, frowning. Then he smiled. "Hey, you're that Capitol detective aren't you? Maybe you can figure out what's haunting this darned machine."

I had solved the mystery of the Demon Cat of Capitol Hill. I didn't know anything about solving electronic mysteries.

"Finally," he said when the machine flashed a green light. He took his coffee and left.

My friend Monica was at the cash register. "Your daddy is working late, eh, Fina?"

"Yup," I said. Papa was always working late. Even after he promised that starting in January, he would be home in time for dinner. It had been January for more than a week now and he still got home about the time I was brushing my teeth and going to bed. Tonight at least we were eating dinner together, but not at home. Instead, we were eating in the Rules Committee office on the third floor of the Capitol.

"Your Papa is the hardest working man in Washington," she said.

I smiled. I liked talking to Monica. Her voice had a purr in it, like she was rolling sounds around in her mouth before they came out. She was from an island in the Caribbean, but she told me the only pirates she ever saw were the ones here in the Capitol. She meant the senators and congress people.

Monica liked to "change it up" as she put it. You never knew what she would look like. Monica always wore wigs, regular ones that looked like real hair, and fun ones like the pink pageboy or the one with 101 braids down the back. I asked why she wore wigs instead of her own hair.

"I wear a uniform for work," she said, tugging on the navy tunic. "But my hair is for me. If I am having a bad day, I wear hair that makes me happy. If I am sad, I have bangs that almost cover my eyes."

I wondered if Papa would let me wear a wig. What I would look like with yellow braids instead of my own dark curls that I kept out of my eyes with a headband?

Tonight Monica's wig had black spikes that stuck out all over the top, like a rock star's. The spikes fluttered as she jerked her head up, listening.

"Do you hear it?" she whispered.

"Hear what?"

"Shh!!"

I heard voices way down the hall and the ding of the elevator bell. I heard the boilers rumbling, trying to keep the Capitol warm in the middle of winter. And I heard – a screech?

"There it is!" Monica said. "Do you hear it?"

"Sounds like a squeaky door," I said.

"Not a door," said Monica. "It is Chickcharney."

"Chick what?" My cup of hot chocolate was getting cold.

"No one believes me. But I have heard it. Chickcharney. It is a bird from my island."

"Okay," I said. "I've got to get back upstairs to Papa."

"I was hoping that you could help me find it."

"Why?"

"I am certain that it carries a message for me. Why else would a bird from my home island of Andros come to the U.S. Capitol?"

"My Papa thinks I should take a break from detecting for a while and concentrate on my homework. I got an 'unsatisfactory' in math on my last report card."

"Please, Fina. You are the only detective I know."

Being a detective was a lot of responsibility.

My sister Gabby said "it figured" when I got into the detecting business since I was always asking questions. She was making a joke, but it was actually true.

"What does it look like?" I asked. "This bird."

"Chickcharney has a round face, a sharp beak, long legs, and a skinny, curly tail."

"You mean curly feathers?"

"No. Chickcharney has a tail like a lizard."

"A lizard tail!" I laughed, imagining just such a bird.

"Shh!" she said. "Chickcharney does not take kindly to those who laugh at him."

"Sorry," I said. "Sorry, Chickcharney."

Monica nodded, satisfied.

"Is this one of those creatures that curses you with bad luck?" I asked.

"Chickcharneys are neither good nor evil. But they are mischief makers. Tricksters. If you respect them, they bring you blessings and good fortune. If you make them angry, a lifetime of misery will follow."

"Why do you want to find this bird if he can make a lifetime of misery for you?"

"I believe he has a message for me," she said. "I believe it is important to find the bird and hear that message."

"There you are!"

It was Papa, wondering what had happened to his sandwich. "I thought there'd be too much for you to carry upstairs by yourself. C'mon. Stop pestering Monica. I've got to get back to work."

"You will think about it, yes?" asked Monica.

"Think about what?" Papa asked.

"Nothing, Papa."

Chapter Two

Papa's office smelled like burnt popcorn. That usually meant one thing.

"Hey, Fina." It was Claudia. Claudia was the "L.A." in Papa's office, the Legislative Assistant who knew everything about everything in the bills voted on by Congress. Papa called her "his brain." Claudia loved popcorn. Especially late at night when she was working with Papa. The only problem was that the office microwave didn't like to work late at night. Instead of popcorn, it turned half the bag into black chunks. Tonight smelled like one of those nights.

"Claudia, did you find those numbers for me?" asked Papa, heading into his back office.

"Right here, congressman." She handed him a page from one of the many folders in her arms. I wish I was super organized like Claudia.

Papa's desk was covered with papers. I sighed. It was going to be a long night. At least it would be the last time I had to wait at Papa's office for him to be done with work. Tomorrow, finally, my grandmother would arrive in Washington to take care of me and my older sister Gabby. We would be a family again. A family without Mama, but a family.

Abuelita was supposed to come with us when we moved from Los Angeles last fall, but she broke her leg and we had to wait until she was able to walk up and down stairs. Abuelita told me her fixed leg made her "faster than ever." I hoped so. Our skinny D.C. row house had lots of stairs.

I plopped down on the couch and peeled my banana. The TV set in the corner was tuned to C-SPAN. It was always tuned to C-SPAN, the world's most boring channel except when Papa was on TV. Tonight, it was what they called "one-minute speeches" when lawmakers asked for permission to talk about anything they wanted, but only for one minute.

Tonight, it was a congressman who sounded like a cowboy. He talked about the "hard working people" in his district who paid too much in taxes. I watched a sentence move across the bottom of the TV screen. It said C-SPAN was going to air the State of the Union on Tuesday night.

"Which state is it?" I asked Claudia.

Claudia looked up from her computer screen.

"Kansas? California?" I guessed.

"What are you talking about?" she asked.

"The State of the Union. Which state?"

I saw that Claudia trying not to laugh. I hated it when people laughed at me. I took a big bite out of the banana.

Claudia apologized. "Sorry, Fina," she said. "It's a fair question. The State of the Union is a speech by the president. It kind of takes the temperature of the country every year."

"Like a checkup on America?"

"Exactly!" she said. "The president comes to the Capitol and reminds Congress about all the good things he did last year and all the things he wants them to do this year. And after the speech, somebody from the other party goes on TV to complain about everything the president just said."

"Is that what Papa is going to do? Complain?"

"Pretty much," she said. "They've been doing it since Lyndon Johnson was president and Senate Republicans wanted a chance to complain about it."

Papa came in waving a piece of paper. "That's what I'll be doing: complaining. In Spanish."

"How do you know what the president is going to say before he says it, Papa?"

"We don't know everything," said Papa, "but it's pretty easy to guess some of the things the president will talk about on Tuesday night. Like immigration. The reason for the rebuttal speech is to present different ideas, from our party's point of view."

Claudia handed Papa a new piece of paper. It was like Claudia knew what he wanted almost before he did. He looked it over, nodded, and went back to his own office.

"Rebuttal?" Sometimes living in Washington, D.C. was like living in a foreign country, with its own language and weird customs like standing on the right side of the escalators to the subway because the left side was for people running to catch their train. Instead of teaching us regular vocabulary words in 4th grade, they should be teaching us a bunch of Washington words like rebuttal.

"Rebuttal means to make an argument that answers back to something," said Claudia.

"Papa's lucky. When I answer back, I get sent to my room."

This time, Claudia did laugh. "Sometimes I think you should be running the country, Fina."

I wasn't sure that I wanted to be the president, or even a member of Congress like Papa. It seemed like most of the job was making speeches and sitting through a bunch of meetings. I didn't like small group discussions at school and I hated talking in front of the whole class.

"It's a big honor to be asked to give the Democratic response," said Claudia. "Your dad has to have a first draft in front of the boss by tomorrow morning."

The boss was the Minority Leader, the top Democrat in the House of Representatives. She kind of reminded me of my second grade teacher Mrs. Watkins who smiled too much.

"Speaking of working," called Papa, "You have homework to do. Get to it, mija!"

I sighed. Homework was everybody's favorite word these days.

"Yes, Papa."

I'd already read my ten pages of "Garvey's Choice" for English class, but I still had some math problems. I always had math problems. I pulled the worksheet out of my backpack, but it was hard to concentrate on a page full of numbers.

I thought about Monica's strange bird, about how her voice shook when she talked about Chickcharney. Was it a real bird? Why was it so important for her to hear its message? My brain started thinking like a detective. I couldn't help it.

"Claudia, could I borrow your laptop?"

"Sure," she said, pulling it out of her gigantic tote bag. Papa said I couldn't use work computers for my schoolwork or he'd get in trouble with the House Ethics Committee. Claudia always brought her own laptop for personal stuff.

"Just don't peek at what I watch on Netflix," she said.

I smiled. I already knew Claudia liked to watch South Korean dramas.

"Chickcharney," I googled. "A legendary creature from the Island of Andros in the Bahamas." Pictures of giant, ugly birds came up, with long legs and dangerous claws. But why would a bird from the Caribbean suddenly show up inside the

U.S. Capitol? Maybe it was a lost pet. There were dogs in the House office buildings, but they belonged to the lawmakers who brought them to work. And there was D.C. the mouse catcher cat in the Capitol Crypt. I didn't know anyone who had a pet bird on Capitol Hill.

"Do you need help with that worksheet?" called Papa from the other office. He knew I wasn't doing homework.

"No, Papa."

I wasn't stupid. I started reading street signs and the back of cereal boxes before I started kindergarten. I beat both Becka and Michael in the class spelling bee. I got an "A" on my science fair project that explained why buildings close to the epicenter, or heart of an earthquake, shook harder and longer than buildings miles away.

But math was like a foreign language to me. My brain froze. I felt like a first grader, secretly counting on my fingers under my desk. Even when I understood the equation, I usually left a number out or made a simple, stupid mistake.

My sister Gabby was great at math. She even took Advanced Placement classes in calculus and statistics at her high school. She tried to help me with my homework. "See? It's easy," she'd say. But it wasn't easy for me.

Papa said, "Don't worry. You'll get it. Eventually." But I was afraid that I would never get it and I would never graduate from fourth grade. I didn't want to be known as the stupid Mendoza. Like I said, I wasn't stupid.

I closed the laptop and stared at my worksheet. How much was eight times nine? And how could I find out more about Chickcharney?

Chapter Three

We were late. Again.

Papa, Gabby and I crammed into the taxi. It was a minivan, but one of the little ones. Traffic got stuck as usual on the 14th Street Bridge, just past the Jefferson Memorial. We could almost see the airport on the other side of the river.

By the time we finally got to the terminal, Abuelita was waiting for us, wearing her red coat, standing by a mountain of luggage. I worried about having enough room in the van. The driver kept saying "no worries" but I couldn't help it.

Abuelita insisted on taking Southwest Airlines, even though she had to change planes in Dallas. "Because you get two free suitcases on Southwest," she told Papa on the phone. "Why should I waste my money?"

Except Abuelita didn't just bring two suitcases. I counted at least five, plus a box wrapped in miles of packing tape. Papa grunted when he lifted it. "What in heaven's name did you pack, Mama?"

"Careful, mijo!" she said. "That's my sewing machine."

Abuelita was moving her whole life to Washington just to help Papa take care of us. We'd been waiting for her to get here since Halloween. Talking to her on the phone just wasn't the same thing. She always asked "what else?" meaning what else was running around in my head? What else was I not telling her? She always knew when my brain was working overtime.

Maybe it was because she had my name: Josefina Mendoza. I guess it was really her name since she had it first. Nobody called me Josefina, unless I was in trouble. Everyone just called me Fina.

Abuelita hugged Papa and planted a kiss on his forehead. It was bright orange. Then, she inspected Gabby and me.

"Qué grandes!" she exclaimed, even though I hadn't grown a quarter of an inch since the last time she saw me and neither had Gabby.

"Hey, Abuelita," said Gabby. "Smile." Gabby started snapping pictures with the smartphone she got for Christmas and immediately started posting them to social media. Abuelita smiled and waved and hammed it up.

Then she turned to me. I got the full hug treatment. I could smell her tangy sunscreen. She was a Californian. Californians wore sunscreen whether there was sunshine or not. I wondered whether she'd still slather it on in D.C. on days like today when the temperature was only about forty degrees.

It took both Papa and the driver to lift the last bag and squeeze it in with the rest of Abuelita's luggage. "Just a few things to eat," she said. "and – oh, my!"

Abuelita grabbed Gabby's hand and started running across the busy road that circled the airport.

"What the – where is she going?" asked Papa.

Abuelita kept her grip on Gabby and didn't stop until she reached a statue in a tiny park across from the terminal.

"Take my picture, take my picture," Abuelita shouted at Gabby.

It was a statue of Ronald Reagan. They named the airport after him. Reagan National Airport. Abuelita loved Ronald Reagan. Even though he was a Republican and Papa was a Democrat, Abuelita called President Reagan her hero. "It was because of him," she always said, "that I became an American citizen and your father became a congressman." Papa used to argue with her, reminding her that it was Congress that passed the immigration bill that made it possible for Abuelita to become a citizen. President Reagan just signed it. Abuelita never listened. As far as she was concerned, Ronald Reagan was the best president we ever had, better even than Abraham Lincoln or George Washington.

The statue looked regular-sized from the car, as if President Reagan was about to step off the concrete sidewalk to catch a plane. But when Abuelita stood next to him, she barely came up to the button on his bronze jacket.

Behind our minivan, traffic was backing up. New cars and taxis were trying to get to the pick-up area, but we were in the way.

"Get back in the car, Gabby," Papa shouted over the honking horns. "Bring your grandmother back here. Now!"

"What?" Gabby shouted back.

Abuelita reached up to take the bronze statue's giant hand and gestured to Gabby to take a million pictures. Finally, she seemed satisfied and the two of them dashed between cars to get back to the taxi.

Papa was not happy. "You could have been run over!" he told her. "You and your beloved granddaughter. What were you thinking?"

"It was el presidente," she said. "He was here to welcome me to Washington."

Gabby and I had worked really hard to make our house on A Street SE sparkle for Abuelita. We even washed the windows – inside and out. Gabby made me do the outside. It was so cold that I worried the glass cleaner would turn to ice.

The only thing Abuelita noticed was our front door. It was bright blue. "Qué suerte!" she said, tapping her knuckles on the door. A blue door is indeed lucky."

Papa had to make three trips to bring in Abuelita's many bags. I was surprised she didn't supervise. Instead, Abuelita headed straight to the kitchen, peeking in cupboards and pulling out drawers. She clucked at our lonesome spice cabinet with its two little jars of cinnamon and red pepper flakes.

"Not even cumin," she said, shaking her head.

Gabby shrugged. "Homework," she shouted as she ran upstairs and slammed her door. Gabby always said she had homework these days, but I think she was really going through her closet. Again. Gabby kept reorganizing her clothes, as if a new shirt or pair of jeans would miraculously appear. They never did.

Abuelita pulled our biggest pot from its cubbyhole under the counter and turned on the stove. "Mijo," she shouted at Papa, "where is my purple bag?"

"I'll get it, Abuelita," I said and grabbed it off the couch. It was heavy. Abuelita unzipped the bag and took out a gigantic, frozen plastic container and put it in the sink. She ran buckets of hot water over it and then dumped the chunk of ice inside into the pot.

"Albondigas soup," she said. "I froze it to make sure the TSA would let me bring it on the plane."

I loved Abuelita's soup full of meatballs and tomatoes and oregano. It had been months and months since we'd tasted her cooking. Abuelita again reached inside the purple bag and brought out another package: homemade tortillas from the little store around the corner from where we lived in Los Angeles. Abuelita had been in our D.C. house for exactly five minutes and already it smelled like Southern California.

Papa kissed Abuelita on her head. He wasn't very tall, but Papa towered over his mama. "Smells wonderful," he said. And then his work phone rang. Papa, like everybody on Capitol Hill, had three phones – one for work, one for home, and one for calling people to ask them for money so that he could run for re-election. When Papa's work phone rang, he usually had to run out the door to a meeting for what he called "crisis control." I knew what was coming next.

"He what?" Papa exploded into the phone. Papa exploded a lot into the phone. "Sorry, Mama. I'll have to eat my soup later. I've got an emergency meeting on the Hill. Be back as soon as I can."

And in a flash, Papa was gone. As usual. The only difference this time was that Gabby and I weren't left alone in the house. Tonight, Abuelita was here with us.

Chapter Four

"But I don't need you to walk me to school, Abuelita. I know the way."

I did not want to show up at Saint Phillip's with my grandmother, like I was a first grader. But Abuelita was buttoning up her red coat and reaching for her hat and gloves.

"You may know the way, but I do not," she said. "What if there is some emergency and I need to come get you at your school? How would I know how to find you?"

"You could ask anyone where Saint Philip School was and they'd tell you."

It wasn't fair. Abuelita treated me like I was a baby. I was almost 11 now. Almost a teenager. I'd been walking myself to school for four whole months. I had a real job, an important job. I walked dogs for members of Congress. Well, one dog. I had unpacked a hundred and two moving boxes, all by myself. Okay, Gabby helped, too. I made toast every morning and pushed the button that started Papa's coffee. I even solved a mystery.

Abuelita thought I was still in pre-school. She probably wanted to hold my hand when we crossed the street. "Please, Abuelita," I begged. "It's not a big deal. It's three blocks. I know my way. You don't have to walk me."

"I don't have to," she replied. "I want to."

And just like that, she grabbed my hand and the house keys and we were out on the sidewalk. She wouldn't even let go of my hand. "Just in case I trip on these crooked sidewalks," she said. "You wouldn't want me to break my other leg, would you?"

I opened my mouth to argue, but the sidewalks were pretty awful in Washington. Tree roots pushed them around so they were never flat. It would be easy for Abuelita to trip and fall. And if Abuelita broke her other leg, Papa would never forgive me. I sighed and started walking, the two Josefinas, walking hand and hand.

The trees were bare now and most of the houses had taken down their Christmas lights weeks ago. "Are you warm enough, Abuelita?" I asked. "Maybe you should head back home before you catch a cold."

"I am fine, mija. Let's just walk a little faster. That will get your California blood moving."

We were getting closer to the school. Someone could see me. Maybe I could explain that we were exercising Abuelita's broken leg, or tell everyone that she was 106 years old instead of just 66 and I had to walk her every day like a dog. Maybe if I kept my head buried in my hoodie, no one would recognize me. Maybe –

"Hey, Fina!"

I looked up. It was Michael, wearing his orange crossing guard vest. "Hi, Michael," I said.

"Who is your friend, the policeman?" asked Abuelita.

Michael stuck out a hand. "Michael Fisher. I'm not a policeman, just a crossing guard. You must be Fina's grandmother."

Abuelita let go of my hand long enough to shake Michael's. Maybe this wasn't going to be so bad. Maybe everyone at school wouldn't find out that Fina Mendoza had to be walked to school by her grandmother. Maybe.

"Hey, Fina," shouted a familiar voice behind me. "Is your nanny taking you to school today?"

It was Becka, my least favorite person in the whole entire world. The first time I met her, Becka told me that her mother worked for a senator and because "everybody knew" that senators were more important than congressmen, she was more important than me. I tried to steer clear of Becka.

"She's not my nanny. She's –"

"I'm your substitute teacher this morning," said Abuelita. My mouth opened wide. Nothing came out of it. Becka seemed suspicious, but

Abuelita put on her "don't mess with me" face and glared at Becka. "And you'd better hurry inside young lady if you don't want to be late. Go on."

Becka hesitated for a moment, but then ran off.

"Are you really our substitute teacher, Ms. Mendoza?" asked Michael.

"No, but I didn't want to embarrass Fina in front of her 'friend.' Perhaps you can take it from here, Mr. Crossing Guard. Escort her the rest of the way. Yes?"

"Sure," said Michael.

Abuelita winked at me, turned around, and marched home.

Abuelita wasn't there after school to walk me to my job. I guess she finally believed Papa that Capitol Hill was the safest place on planet Earth since there were policemen on practically every corner. I skipped all the way down C Street to the Rayburn House Office Building.

Upstairs, I opened the office door that read "Representative Carol Mitchell, Georgia." As usual, everybody in the office was on the phone.

"Let me connect you to our Director of Constituent Services," said the girl on the phone. I knew that meant the person who took care of problems for the people back in Georgia. Papa had a constituent services person, too, for the voters back in his Los Angeles district.

"I'll check her calendar," said another staffer. "No, sorry. She's got a meeting that afternoon." It sounded like Congresswoman Mitchell was as busy as Papa. How many meetings did it take to run the government?

It was noisy in the office, and not just from all the people on the phones. There was a grinding noise coming from somewhere else in the building. It sounded like the drill the dentist used on your teeth when you had a cavity.

I heard the jingle of dog tags and four furry feet flying, and there in front of me was my best friend in Washington, Senator Something.

Senator Something wasn't a real senator. He was a big orange dog, a Briard, a French dog that herded sheep. Senator Something didn't speak French, though.

He jumped up on my school uniform, almost knocking me over. "Well, I'm glad to see you too, Senator Something! How was your Christmas?"

Senator Something had gone to Georgia with the congresswoman when she drove south for the holidays. He must have had a good time. He looked a little fatter.

I grabbed his leash from the coat rack and clipped it to his harness. The girl at the front desk was still on the phone, but she waved back at me as I followed Senator Something out the door.

We walked across the street to the little park on top of the parking garage. There was never anybody there, except the smokers who got chased away from the front entrances of the House office buildings.

After doing his poop business, and after I used the plastic bag to clean it up, we sat on one of the benches. Actually, I sat on the bench. He sat on the ground. The sun was super bright, but it was still cold. Especially the bench.

I told him about my grandmother finally getting here and how she insisted on walking me to school. He whimpered. He knew I was not happy about that. Senator Something was a good listener.

"You remember Monica?" I asked.

He woofed. Monica was one of his favorite people, probably because she always smelled a little bit like the hamburgers they cooked on the grill in the Capitol Carry Out.

"Monica has a case for me, Senator Something. A real mystery. But I need some more information. Wanna come with me?"

Of course he did. Senator Something was a very good partner for a detective.

It was a slow time at the Capitol Carry Out, just past potato-chips-and-Frappuccino breaks and just before dinnertime. Monica wasn't at her cash register. I figured she was eating a late lunch. Monica never ate from the Capitol Carry Out. She always brought her own food to work. I could smell ginger and chili coming from the room across the hall where there was a microwave and a few tables. I parked Senator Something outside and went looking for Monica. I followed my nose, peeking inside the microwave's window. I could see little peas and rice going round and round.

"Pigeon peas," she said.

I turned around and smiled. It was Monica in a bright blue wig.

"Pigeon peas?" I tried to imagine pigeons laying peas instead of eggs.

"They're a kind of pea that grows on my island," she said.

I guessed that Monica was like Abuelita, cooking things that made her think of home.

"How long have you been gone?" I asked. "From your island."

"Long time," she said.

"What was it like?"

She smiled. "Paradise. Andros is always warm, but never hot. There is always a small breeze in the afternoon."

She took her plate out of the microwave and handed me a plastic fork. "Want a bite?"

I did. I stuck a forkful in my mouth and smiled. The peas were a little bit crunchy and tasted a little like nuts. "Yum."

Senator Something stuck his head into the lunch room and whimpered. He looked at Monica with his saddest eyes. She laughed and tossed him a pea. He gulped it down and smacked his lips.

"My mother had a little place where you could get a plate of fried fish and pigeon peas and rice. And a beer," she said. "It was the kind of place where everyone in the neighborhood would come and sit in the yard for hours to eat and drink and catch up on all the gossip."

"What happened to your mother's place?"

"All gone in that hurricane."

Monica took a paper napkin from the container on the table and wiped her eyes. Even Senator Something looked like he might cry.

"I'm sorry," I said.

"But now we are here. And someday, my husband and I, we will open our own little place where we will fry some fish and cook up some rice and peas and everyone will stay for hours and hours and gossip. Someday."

"You'll make a million dollars if you cook like this," I said, pointing my fork at her pigeon peas.

Senator Something barked in agreement.

She smiled. "That is why I work extra hours. To save up the money."

She lowered her voice. "And why I must hear the message from Chickcharney."

"Chickcharney is going to help you start a restaurant?"

"Not exactly," she said. "But his message, I am sure it is from my mother."

"Why don't you just call her?"

"I wish that I could. My mother, she is late."

The pigeon peas felt like a rock in my stomach. Monica didn't mean that her mama had missed the bus and was late coming to meet her. She meant that her mama had died.

My mama had died.

Mama. I used to think about her every single day. Now, I only thought about her sometimes. Did Mama think I was forgetting her? Impossible! But it was hard to remember her voice when she called me "Fina Finay." Mama. If my Mama had a message for me, I would want to hear it, too. Just like Monica.

And then I had a thought: was it possible that Chickcharney had a message for me, too? From Mama?

That was silly. Why would Mama send a bird to deliver a message? Besides, I didn't even know if the bird was real. But still…

"Do you have any proof," I asked Monica, "that Chickcharney is really here?"

She looked around the room, then leaned in and whispered. "Every night, I leave out food for him. Every morning when I come to work, the plate is empty."

I didn't say it to Monica, but it was more likely the janitors threw out the food every night.

"Will you do this thing for me, Fina? Will you find Chickcharney?"

I looked at Senator Something. He nodded his head. He agreed. I needed to help Monica. And maybe just maybe, Chickcharney would have a message for me, too.

"I will try," I said.

But how?

I took Senator Something back to his office and walked home with Papa. Before Abuelita got here, we did that every night. Not anymore. It was nice to have him to myself again for a few blocks, walking past the Library of Congress. I opened my mouth to tell him about my Chickcharney investigation, about how I was helping Monica, but the fundraising phone rang.

It was the DCCC, the Democratic Congressional Campaign Committee. They called to remind Papa about the meeting for his fundraiser.

It cost a lot to be a congressman. Papa was always looking for money to help pay for lawn signs and bumper stickers and donuts for the volunteers who went door to door to register voters and ask them to vote for Arturo Mendoza. Volunteers ate a lot of donuts.

Politics was all about food sometimes. For the fundraiser, Papa invited all the best chefs from all the best food trucks in L.A. to come to Washington and cook for the people who would give him money to run for re-election. I hoped I'd get invited. I also hoped I wouldn't have to spend any of my dog-walking money to go to the fundraiser.

I never got the chance to tell Papa about my latest case. He talked and talked on the phone all the way home. When I opened the front door, it looked like some kind of hurricane had hit the living room. The couch was covered with stacks of sweaters and piles of polo shirts. Or rather, pieces of sweaters and shirts. Safety pins were scattered everywhere. Bits of fabric and thread covered the floor. Abuelita's sewing machine sat in the middle of the dining room table. Gabby was sitting right in front of it.

"What's going on in here, mija?" asked Papa.

"I'm fixing my clothes," said Gabby, "since you don't give me enough allowance to buy anything new."

Gabby had been complaining about her allowance since she turned sixteen.

"You wear a uniform to school," said Papa. "How many clothes do you need?"

"We have free dress day once a month and I can't keep wearing the same things."

Gabby was cutting off sleeves from her old sweaters and making holes in her jeans on purpose.

"What are you looking at?" she asked.

"Nothing," I said and went upstairs. When Gabby was in a crabby mood, it was better to be somewhere else.

There had been lots of changes to our rented house on A Street SE since Abuelita arrived. She couldn't paint the walls, but Abuelita decided she should change everything else.

Mysterious boxes started arriving. Out went the curtains in the kitchen, the front room, even our bedrooms. In came yards and yards of fabric. One kind had sunflowers and bees that made you smile. It went in the kitchen. Abuelita covered the living room windows in a soft, green velvety fabric that touched the floor. She kept reminding me not to touch it unless I'd just washed my hands. "I don't want peanut butter all over those drapes!" That's what she called them. Drapes. I liked the fringy part on the bottom. They tickled my fingers when I rubbed them across the twisted strings.

Abuelita put rubber mats on the kitchen shelves and bought a new toothbrush holder and a furry bathmat for the bathroom. She ordered everything online.

"I think your middle name is Amazon," Papa told her.

The one thing Abuelita couldn't change was our lucky front door. She found out that in Washington, blue was a Democratic color. Red was for Republicans. Abuelita was no Democrat. She and Papa used to argue sometimes about politics until Mama told them to "knock it off." To Abuelita, our blue front door was a daily reminder that she lived in a Democratic house.

There was almost a big fight between Abuelita and Papa, but it wasn't about politics. It started when Abuelita decided to move the furniture around. It wasn't our furniture. It came with the house. She pushed the sofa over by the front window and dragged two big armchairs across the living room so that they were closer to the fireplace. She stuck the ugly end table down at the end of the long downstairs hallway.

Then she went upstairs and brought down something wrapped in tissue paper. It was a photograph in a fancy gold frame, a picture of Mama in her blue graduation gown, taken on the day that she finished law school.

We didn't have any pictures of Mama hanging on our walls or sitting on our bookshelves. They made Papa too sad. Some nights, when Papa was working late at the office, Gabby and I would open the laptop and look at old pictures stored on the G drive, going through them one by one. They were pictures of our old life, back in Los Angeles, when Mama was still alive.

Abuelita put the photograph of Mama on the table at the end of the hallway. It was exactly the same place where Gabby and I had made a Dia de los Muertos altar last fall. We had covered the table with a lacy pillowcase and a little vase of flowers Gabby "borrowed" from the house next door, and a brownie and the sports section of the newspaper. In the center, we put our favorite picture of Mama. We took the altar apart before Papa could see it.

What would he say when he saw Abuelita's little altar?

It took a couple of days for Papa to notice.

"What is that, Mama?" he asked, pointing.

"The table looks so much better here," she said, not mentioning the picture of Mama.

Papa opened his mouth to say something. Gabby and I held our breath. Papa closed his mouth. He never mentioned it again.

Tonight, while Papa was on the phone and Abuelita and Gabby were washing dishes, I crept down the hallway to the little table. I gently touched the picture. "Do you have a message for me, Mama?"

She didn't answer. But maybe Chickcharney would.

Chapter Five

Every member of Congress got to bring one person to the State of the Union address.

"Usually, you pick a guest to make a point about an issue you care about, like gun control or small business growth or education," said Papa. "Tonight, I'm making a point about family. We are finally a family, here together at last."

Well, sort of. Gabby didn't want to come. She wasn't interested in politics, she told Papa as often as he would listen. So Abuelita got Papa's ticket and Congresswoman Mitchell gave me hers. She was kind of my boss. She paid me five dollars a day to walk Senator Something. When she handed me my money last week, she also handed me a fancy cardboard ticket for the State of the Union speech.

"It's like gold," she told me. "Don't lose it."

Of course, I did lose it. Papa said it was because I wasn't thinking about "the task at hand." The good news was that Gabby found the ticket next to the bathroom sink. I must have left it there when I was brushing my teeth.

Papa told us to wear our nicest clothes. That meant the Christmas dress that Abuelita had sewn for me. It was bright red, which was okay, but it had old-fashioned ruffles on the skirt and it itched. I felt stupid, like I was wearing a costume in a school play. I wanted to wear my school uniform, but Abuelita said this was an important night and I needed to "dress the part." She meant that I had to look like the daughter of the man who was going to be on TV after the State of the Union speech to tell America all the things that the president said that were wrong, and say them in Spanish.

Abuelita held onto her State of the Union ticket so hard, I thought she'd tear it. My shoes pinched as we walked over to the Capitol. I hadn't worn the shiny black church shoes since last Easter. Now they were too small.

I showed Abuelita what to do as we walked through a bunch of security checkpoints, putting her house keys and my jangly bracelets in the little plastic tub of the X-ray machine and walking through the metal detector. Finally, we got up to the House gallery, the balcony over the House floor. The stairs in the gallery were really steep, and I worried that Abuelita would fall over the edge and land on the lawmakers down below.

Papa told us that we'd have to run back up those stairs to get out of the gallery before the end of the speech. "Keep an eye on the guys in the press area," Papa said. "They get a paper copy of the speech. When the president gets to the second to the last page, your job is to leave the gallery and get down here before the president is done."

"Why?" I asked.

"When the president is on the move, the Secret Service locks down the place," said Papa. "If you get stuck, they won't let you leave the gallery until he's safely in his limousine heading back to the White House. If you want to hear my speech, you've got to get down here before they lock you in."

As soon as Abuelita and I sat down, I looked over at the reporters. Nobody had the paper copy of the speech yet. They were busy talking into microphones, describing what they could see and telling people on TV and radio what they thought the president would talk about in his speech.

The reporters weren't the only ones talking. Down on the House floor, there was a kind of roar, with lawmakers talking over each other. It was more crowded than usual. Usually, senators stayed on their side of the Capitol. But tonight, all one hundred of them came over here to crowd into the extra chairs on the House floor for the president's speech. Except none of them were sitting down. They stood around, pounding each other on the back and shaking a lot of hands. And just like when the House members were there all by themselves, the Republican senators were on one side of the chamber and the Democrats were over on the other side.

Our seats were right above the Republican chairs. I spotted Congresswoman Mitchell. She must have felt my eyes on her because she looked up and waved at me. I waved back, but then worried that I might get into trouble. I wasn't sure whether you were supposed to wave at people on the House floor.

The back door to the chamber opened and a bunch of people walked in. "That's the cabinet," I told Abuelita. "They work for the president."

After the cabinet, some generals marched in, wearing uniforms covered in ribbons and pins. A group wearing black choir robes came next. It was the Supreme Court. And then I saw her, with her curly black hair and black framed glasses and yes, even her jangly bracelets just like mine!

"Hola, Justice Sotomayor!" It was Abuelita.

We were in trouble now. Abuelita loved Justice Sotomayor, but I knew that shouting at people on the House floor was definitely not okay. Papa gave me a list of rules when I showed him my ticket. "No laughing unless everyone is laughing and it's a real joke. No doing anything to call attention to yourself. And no talking."

Abuelita wasn't just talking. She was shouting.

"Nosotras te amamos!"

I loved Justice Sotomayor, too. But I wasn't sure that I wanted every member of Congress and all of the generals and everybody watching on TV to know that.

"Shh, Abuelita!" I whispered, tugging on her dress to try to get her to sit back down. She didn't sit. I looked around to see if there was a Capitol policeman coming to take us away.

But then, Justice Sotomayor looked up at the people in the gallery. Abuelita waved.

"Don't do that, Abuelita," I whispered.

She wouldn't listen. She kept waving. Just as the other justices were sitting down, Sonia Sotomayor waved back at Abuelita, her many bracelets clinking so loud that I could hear them up here. I couldn't believe it!

"Close your mouth, Fina," whispered Abuelita. "You're catching flies."

I loved my grandmother, but sometimes I wished she wasn't my grandmother. Tonight I wished she was just some stranger sitting next to me. I pretended that I was a tourist and this was the first time I'd ever visited Washington, D.C. I looked at the old fashioned lights by the doors and the giant American flag behind the chair where the Speaker sat. I stared up at the ceiling. I guess I never looked up all the other times I'd watched Papa give speeches on the House floor. There was an eagle up there. Not a real eagle, just one made out of white glass. It wasn't very pretty, but it was plenty big. I stared at it so long that I thought I heard it screech.

"Yeah, right," I told myself. "Glass eagles don't screech."

"Screech."

I turned to Abuelita. "Did you hear that?"

"Hear what, mija?"

Suddenly, there was a buzz around us and a lot of people stood up. Was the president finally here?

Nope. It was his wife. Just a few rows to the left of us, the First Lady carefully walked down those steep steps in really high heels. She was wearing a green dress the color of money, with a row of shiny gold buttons down the front. Her two little boys wore First Communion suits. I wondered if they would cause trouble during the speech.

It got really quiet and a bald man with a loud voice announced, "Mr. Speaker, the President of the United States."

There was a lot of cheering on one side of the House floor and some polite clapping on the other side.

The back door opened again, and the president walked in. He didn't get very far because he had to shake hands with all the lawmakers who sat at the ends of the rows of chairs. "Claudia told me they had to get there by lunchtime if they wanted to save those seats," I whispered to Abuelita. "I think they just want to be on TV."

Finally, the president made his way to the microphone and started talking. It was a long speech about a lot of stuff. He even talked about immigration, or at least how he didn't want Congress messing around with it. "No amnesty, ever," he said.

Abuelita grumbled under her breath. It was a good thing the president didn't speak Spanish.

The president pointed to soldiers and nurses and farmers sitting in the seats around us and told stories about them. People applauded. I yawned.

"Don't fall asleep," Abuelita whispered.

It wasn't just because the speech was boring. It was late. The president didn't even start talking until after my bedtime. I decided I could keep my eyes busy by counting how many times people applauded and see who was doing the clapping, the Democrats or the Republicans. One time – I think it was when the president mentioned veterans trying to get better health care – both sides clapped. But just that one time.

And then it happened. Right when the president raised his arm to point to another person in the gallery, something fell from the ceiling. It landed right in the middle of the president's fluffy hair.

"What the ..." The president patted his head. His perfectly hair-sprayed hair looked as crunchy as a bird's nest. He looked at his hand. He smelled his hand. He made a face.

"Screech!"

Everybody looked up. It was a bird.

There was a great hush on the House floor. And then one lawmaker shouted, "Get that bird!"

Secret Service agents ran onto the House floor and surrounded the president. Lawmakers started talking loudly, pointing at the ceiling. People sitting in the gallery looked up, shouting, "I think it flew over there" and "there's a feather!"

A bird. A trickster. Could it be Monica's Chickcharney?

"Let's go," whispered Abuelita.

"But–"

"Now," she said. "¡Ándale!" She jumped up and crawled over three people in our row, dragging me behind her.

"Excuse me," I said to everybody, but I could tell they were mad at us.

We climbed up the steep concrete steps and ran out the upper doors. Abuelita moved pretty fast for someone who had broken her leg not so many months ago. I pushed the button on the elevator.

"Not the elevators," she said.

Instead, we scrambled down the wide marble staircase. There were dips in the middle from all the lawmakers who ran up and down those same steps over the years. We ran past the giant painting of a wagon train with the guy on a horse pointing straight ahead. We ran past the Capitol police guarding the hallway below, flashing our family passes. There were sure a lot of police tonight. We

ran past the doorway to Statuary Hall where reporters and TV cameras and bright lights and miles
of cable filled every inch of space. The reporters
were waiting for lawmakers to come out and say
something about the president's speech.

"Hey," shouted one reporter to us. "What happened in there?"

But we couldn't stop. We had to hurry. Papa
said we'd be locked out if we weren't in the room
when he started talking on TV.

We found the room labeled H-230 and opened
the door. Inside, Papa was sitting in a leather chair,
next to an American flag. There was always an
American flag nearby whenever someone from
Congress went on TV.

Papa was looking over his notes. His glasses
reflected the bright TV lights. His face was plastered with tons of makeup.

"Arturo!" Abuelita called. "We made it!"

A dozen people shushed her, even the makeup
girl.

"We go live in two minutes!" said a woman
with headphones and a little microphone, the kind
football coaches used on game day.

"Here. Sit over here, you two," said a man with
a clipboard.

We were ushered over to a couch in the corner
where you could almost see Papa.

"Here we go in three, two, one ..."

"Buenas noches," said Papa as he introduced himself to people watching him on Univision. "Soy Congresista Arturo Mendoza."

No bird dropped poop on Papa's head. In fact, he never even mentioned the bird. Instead, he talked about immigration. He talked about the good things immigrants brought to this country, about the hard work they did and the small businesses they started. He didn't talk as long as the president. But Papa looked like a president.

I sat there thinking about what it would be like to live in the White House. If Papa was president, I'd probably be surrounded by a hundred Secret Service agents, even in school. That would make Becka mad. But if I was a First Daughter, I probably wouldn't be able to walk Senator Something any more. I wondered whether Senator Something was watching TV tonight.

And then it was over. People in the room applauded, Abuelita the loudest of all. She gave Papa a kiss and ended up with sticky makeup on her face. She used her handkerchief to wipe it off, then she wiped it off Papa.

"So, how'd I do, mija?" he asked.

"Super, Papa! I wish I could be as brave as you when I have to stand up in front of the class. How do you do it?"

"Practice, mija. Practice."

There was a party after Papa's speech in a room outside the Minority Leader's office. Even if I didn't know where the party was, I probably could have found it just by following the noise. People were talking and laughing and a band was playing an old-fashioned disco song.

Abuelita whistled when she peeked inside the room. There were two fireplaces and the usual gigantic chandeliers and even that painting of George Washington from my history book. "Pretty fancy, Fina," she said.

I didn't see Papa, but Claudia saw us. She waved us over. "Fina! I almost didn't recognize you in your fabulous finery."

It wasn't fabulous. The dress was still scratchy. Abuelita kept telling me that if I didn't keep my hands off the ruffle, she would cut it off. The ruffle, she meant, not my hands.

"And this must be Mrs. Mendoza."

It seemed strange to hear Abuelita called Mrs. Mendoza. And sad. That was my mom's name. Mama would loved to have been here tonight. She would have been so proud of Papa. But Mama never moved to Washington with us. We buried her back in California. So I guess Abuelita was the only Mrs. Mendoza now. I cleared my throat, the way Papa did when he was going to introduce somebody important.

"Claudia, this is my Abuelita."

"A pleasure," said Claudia. "I've heard so much about Fina's grandmother."

"Do not believe a word of it," said Abuelita with a smile. "And you are the owl woman who knows how to make my son even smarter."

"I don't know about that," said Claudia. "Owl woman?" she whispered to me.

"I think it's because of your glasses," I whispered back. Claudia did look a little bit like an owl. Her brownish eyes looked gigantic behind the lenses.

Claudia smiled her "polite to strangers" smile and asked, "Can I get you something to drink? A glass of wine? Some lemonade?"

"Lemonade for two would be very nice," said Abuelita.

Claudia walked over to the bar. People in the room were talking about the bird pooping on the president.

"Must have been a Democratic bird," said one man.

"Guess the speech laid an egg," said a woman.

"Maybe they should call it the State of the Omelet speech."

Abuelita looked around the room, scrunching her face to see better. Her glasses were in her purse because she said she didn't want to look like an old lady on her first night at the Capitol.

A man in a white shirt and a little bow tie walked by with a tray of little pieces of toast with stuff on top. He offered them to Abuelita, and then to me. They smelled like fish.

"No thanks," I said. I wasn't a big fish fan, and I was afraid that the thing sitting on top of the bread would land on my dress.

People started clapping and cameras started flashing as a skinny lady entered the room. "She's the boss," whispered Claudia, "the Minority Leader."

Abuelita looked at me to translate.

"Papa's party didn't win enough seats in the last election to be in charge of Congress, so he's in the minority party," I told Abuelita. "If they do better next time, that lady could be the Speaker of the House."

"She reminds me of La Reina," said Abuelita. I wasn't sure the Minority Leader would like to be compared to Abuelita's lucky Queen of Hearts. She took that playing card with her whenever she went to the Indian casinos. It was her good luck charm.

"Ladies and gentlemen," said the Minority Leader. "Tonight, the president delivered a report card on how he thinks we're doing as a nation. If you ask me, I would give the president a D minus!"

I didn't think it was a very funny joke. But everyone in the room laughed. I guess they had to laugh. She was their boss.

She introduced a few people and then said, "Our excellent response 'en Español' was delivered by the Honorable Arturo Mendoza from my home state of California."

That was when Abuelita put her glasses on so that she could see Papa shake the Minority Leader's hand. People clapped again. More cameras flashed.

"Tutu!" called Abuelita. That was the name she used to call Papa when he was a little boy. "Tutu!"

Papa turned red.

"Bienvenidos, 'Tutu,'" said the Minority Leader. Some of the party guests who'd probably had more than two glasses of wine started chanting, "Tutu, Tutu, Tutu." Now I felt my face turning red.

Papa waved at the crowd and walked over to us. He started to muss my hair, but Abuelita stopped him. "I spent twenty minutes combing out the tangles this afternoon. Do you want your daughter to look like a frightened bird on television?"

"I'm not going to be on television, Abuelita," I said.

"You never know," said Abuelita, looking around the room at all the cameras.

"True enough," said Papa. "And how do I look, Mama?"

Papa's hair was slicked down, the way he liked it when he was on TV. I looked closer. He still looked kind of orangey.

"Handsome as ever," said Abuelita.

A man came up and slapped Papa on the back and shook his hand. Papa introduced Abuelita and the man shook her hand. I didn't want to shake hands. I was tired.

I went over to the dessert table and tried to choose between the cake pops on a stick or the cookie in the shape of a donkey.

"Hey, Fina!"

It was Michael from school.

"Michael! What are you doing here?"

Michael pointed across the room. His dad was a TV reporter, interviewing the Minority Leader.

"Did they catch it?" he asked.

"Catch what?"

"The bird. The one that pooped on the president. It's a great story. Nobody will remember anything the president said in his speech. Tomorrow, everybody will be wondering about that bird."

I wondered about that bird, too. Was it Chickcharney? Should I tell the Secret Service about the legend of that bird from the Bahamas? Would they believe me?

"Michael, what do you think the Secret Service or the Capitol police will do to that bird if they catch it?"

"Shoot it, probably," he said.

Shoot it! The poor bird.

And then I had another thought: if they killed the bird, Monica would never hear its message. Neither would I.

I needed to consult my partner in detection. I needed to talk to Senator Something.

Chapter Six

The president was really mad about the bird poop. He demanded that Congress start an immediate investigation. "Find that bird!" he tweeted.

"Check this out, Fina," said Gabby at breakfast. She held out her phone, showing me all these funny gifs on social media. There were short videos of birds pooping on everything they didn't like: broccoli, traffic tickets, the Houston Astros. There was even a TikTok video of eggs being laid in a nest that looked a lot like the president's hair.

"The State of the Union bird even has its own Twitter hashtag," she said. "PoopOnPOTUS."

POTUS was short for president of the United States. Everything in Washington had a regular name and an alphabet name.

Abuelita was watching the political guys on cable TV argue while she made breakfast. "I'm waiting for them to talk about your Papa's speech," she told me, pointing to the screen.

Papa poured himself a cup of coffee. "You could be waiting a long time. The only people who talk about the State of the Union rebuttal en Español are on Spanish language TV."

Papa was right. The political guys didn't mention his speech. They didn't even argue about the president's speech. Instead, they yakked on and on about what kind of bird had interrupted the State of the Union address. "Gotta be an eagle," one guy said. "An eagle is presidential. A noble bird. Our national bird." The TV showed about a million pictures of patriotic eagles. The other guy on TV wasn't so sure. "Could just be a pigeon," he laughed, cackling like a hen.

Or something else, I thought. It could be Chickcharney.

The TV guys said the football team in Philadelphia was sending the president a helmet with eagle wings painted on it to protect him from future bird attacks.

"Hah," said Papa, reading *The Washington Post*. "Here's a letter to the editor. Some eagle dive-bombed a drone a few months back. This guy is worried an eagle will dive-bomb the presidential helicopter when it lifts off from the White House lawn."

A commercial came on TV for the Washington hamburger chain whose French fries were big and soggy. "We've got 'em," the commercial announced. "Executive Eagle Burgers!"

"That doesn't sound very patriotic," said Abuelita. "Eating the national bird."

"They aren't actual eagles, Abuelita," said Gabby. "They're just chicken sandwiches."

Even if they were just chicken, I still didn't want an eagle burger.

At school, we talked about eagles, too. Ms. Greenwood showed us the website for the Bald Eagles who lived in the National Arboretum, a giant park with lots of trees. The male bird was named Mr. President. The female didn't have a name yet. There was a camera pointed at their nest. It was more sticks than straw, like a little fort sitting in a tree. It was also empty. Ms. Greenwood said the eggs wouldn't be laid until spring.

In the background, you could hear a crow cawing and even a bee buzzing. But there were also the city sounds of Washington, D.C. with sirens in the background and a car that sounded like Tío Tom's before he fixed it.

Finally, there was a rush of wings and an eagle flew into the picture. A second bird landed. Their claws were sharp and they had a mean look on their faces. Maybe not mean. Fierce "don't mess with me" faces. They didn't look bald. They looked like they were wearing white football helmets.

We watched for a while and then Ms. Greenwood talked about how the Bald Eagle became a symbol of our country.

"The Continental Congress asked Benjamin Franklin, Thomas Jefferson, and John Adams to design an emblem, a sort of avatar for what would become the United States. It took three committees and the Secretary of Congress to finally come up with a design. And that design included a Bald Eagle."

Ms. Greenwood said Benjamin Franklin thought it was the wrong kind of bird for America. He even wrote a letter to his sister, calling the Bald Eagle a "bird of bad moral character" since it waited around until some other bird caught a fish, and then stole it. "Franklin said a turkey would have been a better American bird," said Ms. Greenwood.

I wondered what we'd be eating on Thanksgiving if Benjamin Franklin had gotten his way.

"Because the Bald Eagle is our national symbol, eagles can be found all over Washington," said Ms. Greenwood. "Your assignment: find some of those eagles. And write a three paragraph report about them."

That was easy. I already knew about the eagle in the ceiling over the House floor. And I remembered a second eagle that sat on top of a metal stick next to the Speaker's chair. Papa told me the stick was called a mace. I'd write about them. I wondered if there were more eagles inside the Capitol.

Ms. Greenwood gave us time to do research on our laptops. I went straight to the AOC website, the Architect of the Capitol. He was in charge of all the murals and statues in the U.S. Capitol. The website said there was a wooden eagle covered in gold in the old Senate chamber. And in Statuary Hall, that big room where all the reporters hung out the night of the State of the Union, there was a statue of Lady Liberty with an eagle on one side of her and a snake on the other. I thought that meant good and evil, but the AOC website said that a serpent meant wisdom.

There was even a big eagle on the Capitol itself. Sort of. On top of the Capitol dome, there was another statue, this one of a lady named Freedom who wore a helmet with a dead eagle on top. The feathers stuck up all around and the bird's feet hung down by her face. You can't see that from the ground, but there was a plaster statue of her in the Capitol Visitor Center. I'd take a closer look at her after school, when I was walking Senator Something. It would also give me a chance to look for Chickcharney.

Things were really busy on Capitol Hill. Claudia said the president told the head of the Capitol police that she was "responsible for maintaining order in the U.S. Capitol." In other words, making sure birds weren't pooping on him during the State of the Union address.

"Practically everyone on Capitol Hill is out looking for that bird," said Claudia.

I heard voices and peeked out the front door of Papa's office. A pair of Capitol policemen were shining their flashlights up at the ceiling, chirping to each other on their walkie-talkies.

"Clear on Cannon 5th floor," said one of them. "We're heading down to the 4th floor next. Over."

"They're bird hunting?"

"Yup," said Claudia. "They've been up and down this hall twice already this afternoon. All this fuss for a stupid bird."

"Will they shoot it?"

"I can't imagine them taking shooting practice inside the Capitol."

That made me feel better.

"What they should do," said Claudia, "is just open the doors and let the bird fly away. All it did was poop, the poor thing."

I looked at the clock. I had to go. "I'm off to my dog walking job," I told Claudia.

"A different sort of poop," she laughed.

Senator Something wanted to walk in the plaza on the east side of the Capitol. It's the place where all the tourists stand in line before they go through the metal detectors just inside the doors to the Capitol Visitor Center. Senator Something wasn't interested in the tourists. He was interested in their leftover lunches. Tourists can't bring food into the Capitol. If they forgot, the Capitol police made them throw their apples and chips into the garbage can at the front of the line. Senator Something would try to get them to feed the leftovers to him instead.

Today, the tourists were throwing their chips and bread crusts all over the plaza, trying to attract the president's bird. Little kids pointed at the sky, shouting, "Look out! Incoming poop!"

"Claudia was right," I told Senator Something. "Looks like everybody is looking for that eagle. Come on. Let's go look at the one on that statue of Freedom."

I flashed my family pass and walked Senator Something through the metal detector. It beeped, of course, but the policemen waved us through. Inside, we stared at the gigantic statue. Senator Something looked at me, puzzled.

"I know," I said. "She really does look silly with a dead bird on her head."

Senator Something agreed with a "woof."

I looked closely at the eagle and shook my head. "You know, Senator Something, everybody is looking for the eagle that pooped on the president. I think it's the same bird Monica wants me to find. Chickcharney."

Senator Something looked at me. I knew he was reminding me that a good detective didn't jump to conclusions. A good detective did her research and asked questions and looked for clues.

"You're right, Senator Something. That's just a hunch. Let's review what we know so far."

I pulled a notebook out of my backpack. It had a smooth brown leather cover, a Christmas present from Claudia. "For your detective work," she'd said.

It was my case book. That was what I called it. Gabby called it my "diary." It's not. A diary was where you wrote down the names of all the boys you had a crush on or complained about how unfair Abuelita was when she decided it was your turn to unload the dishwasher. Again.

I didn't write anything like that in my case book. It was for my investigations. I wrote down all of the information I had about Monica's bird. I showed Senator Something the notes about Chickcharney being a mischief maker. Certainly pooping on the president was mischief. I told him that Monica thought Chickcharney had a special message for her. I didn't tell him that maybe the bird had a message for me, too. It was my secret, my secret with Mama.

"Let's start where Monica first saw Chickcharney," I said. "The basement."

Senator Something barked in agreement. He was a good partner. He kept me focused on solving the case. We walked through the door that read "staff only," past the TV studios where the House Speaker had his weekly news conferences, past the bathrooms, past the circular staircase that went down to the underground meeting rooms, into a hallway that led to the old part of the Capitol. I felt a tight tug on the leash. Senator Something smelled something!

We turned right, then left, then left again. Finally, he stopped.

Of course he did. Senator Something looked at me with a big goofy grin on his face. We were outside the Carry Out. He smelled hamburgers.

"I don't think so," I told him.

Senator Something wasn't supposed to eat anything but kibble these days because he was getting kind of fat. Or at least Congresswoman Mitchell thought he was. Her staffer John said every time Congresswoman Mitchell went on a diet, so did Senator Something. The big orange dog gave me a look that said he was insulted and he wasn't fat. It was just that he needed a haircut.

Inside the Carry Out, Monica heard my voice. She turned around and waved. This afternoon, she wore a giant Afro wig. She said something to another worker who took over her cash register and rushed out to us in the hallway.

"You have news?"

I sighed. "Not yet. But half of Capitol Hill is out looking for the eagle that pooped on the president. They should be catching Chickcharney any minute now."

"But it's not my bird," she said. "My bird is not an eagle. It's not Chickcharney."

"How can you be sure?"

"I have seen him. Last night. After I closed my register. I walked out into the hallway and there he was!" She pointed past the doorway.

"What did he look like?"

"Small," she said. "But the legs! So very long." She gestured to show me just how long those bird legs were. "Eagles do not have long legs."

Was Monica right? Was the bird that pooped on the president a different bird? Were there two birds in the Capitol? Two birds seemed even more impossible than just one.

"Ms. Prosper," said a deep voice, "I thought you already took your afternoon break."

It was Monica's boss. He wore a sour face and a white shirt with the sleeves rolled up.

"Sorry, Mr. Banks. I'll be right there." She waited until her boss had ducked back into the little office next to the cooler. "You do believe me, don't you Fina?" she whispered.

I did believe Monica. I had to find that bird. I had to make sure Chickcharney delivered his message to Monica. And maybe to me. I kept detecting.

After dinner that night, I told Gabby that I needed the laptop. "Research," I said.

I'd already written my report on all the eagles in the U.S. Capitol and I could work on my fractions at breakfast. I had to see if Monica was right.

Monica was convinced that her bird was not an eagle. I googled pictures of eagles and studied them closely. The real ones looked a lot like the eagle statues in the Capitol. They didn't look much like the Chickcharney that Monica described. She was right. Eagle legs were too short. Monica was very clear about that.

Was it possible that there a long-legged eagle? I flipped through the gigantic "Sibley Field Guide to Birds" book that Gabby brought home from the library and looked at all of the eagles and their descriptions. None of them had long legs.

I wanted one more look at a real live eagle, just to be sure that Chickcharney wasn't a cousin. I clicked on the Eagle Cam. It was dark up in those branches and I couldn't see the birds. I figured they were sleeping in their nest. Listening, it was almost like camping, without the mosquitos and the s'mores. You could hear the wind in the trees and a car horn honking in the background and a clicking noise. Was the tree moving in the wind? Or was it another bird? Or...

"Bedtime, Fina," said Papa, sticking his head through the doorway. "You're done with your homework?"

"Almost, Papa." It was mostly true. I didn't mention the fractions I didn't finish. I didn't want Papa to get mad that I was still detecting when I only got a 64 on my last math quiz. "We have to research eagles," I said, showing him the Eagle Cam.

"Save it for tomorrow. Time for lights out. Okay?"

"Okay, Papa. Love you."

"You too, Fina."

"Goodnight, Mr. President and lady bird," I said to the eagles. I yawned and closed the laptop. That night I dreamed that a giant bird with a lizard's tail was sitting on my chest.

"You think you're so smart, Fina Mendoza," the bird said to me, turning its ugly head to the side to stare at me with one eye. He looked like an eagle, but his legs were as long as a stork's.

"Bird brained is more like it," said the creature. "Good luck, girl detective."

I woke up to find that the heavy bird book was still there, squishing my chest.

Chapter Seven

At breakfast, Papa was jingling the change in his pocket, something he always did when he was excited about something.

"What is it, Papa?" I asked. He'd been on the phone a lot since the night of the State of the Union.

Papa just smiled and said nothing.

I still had those four fraction problems to finish before school, but it was hard to concentrate with Papa jingling coins.

"Arturo!" scolded Abuelita.

"Sorry, Mama," he said and winked at me.

I pushed my plate of peanut butter raisin toast away and took out my pencil. I was always scrambling to finish my math homework. It wasn't fair. Papa was a genius in math and Gabby was taking all those Advanced Placement classes. Why was I such a dummy?

Papa looked over my shoulder at the chicken scratches that Ms. Greenwood always insisted we turn in with our homework. They weren't real scratches from chickens, just all the scribbles and crossed-out formulas we used to figure out the answers. She said she wanted to see our work, not just the results.

"Right there, mija," said Papa. "Step three. That's where you went wrong."

I looked at step three. He was right. I corrected my mistake and the rest of the problems were easy. Pretty easy, anyway.

Papa planted a kiss on my forehead and tugged on Gabby's hair.

"Hey," she protested, looking up briefly from her phone.

"Adios, Mama," he said, kissing Abuelita's cheek. "Happy Valentine's Day." He put an envelope in her pocket. "I'll be home late tonight."

"How late, mijo?" she asked.

"Late, late. No dinner for me."

And he was gone. Papa, man of mystery.

Abuelita sighed, but she smiled when she opened her card. It had a big pink heart on the front. A valentine.

"He remembered," she said. "Even when he is busy, he remembered."

I hated Valentine's Day. You had to bring a box of valentines to school – one for everybody in the class. Even one for the people you didn't like very much and who certainly were NOT your valentine.

First we had to learn about Saint Valentine in religion class. He helped a lot of blind people see again. Then the Romans killed him because he kept doing weddings for Christian couples. He was the patron saint of engaged people, people who faint, travelers, and bee keepers. I could understand the engaged people part, but who decided he'd be a good saint for beekeepers and people who faint?

After the saint lesson, we passed around our valentines. I gave store-bought ones to everybody but Michael. For him, I had made a special valentine with lots of glitter. He wasn't exactly my valentine, but he was nicer to me than anyone else in class. He gave me a little box of candy hearts with sayings on them. Mine said "PurrFect" and "Whiz Kid."

Becka brought fancy cupcakes from the store in Georgetown where you had to wait in a line that stretched around the block. They tasted okay, but there was too much frosting. I liked Abuelita's cupcakes better.

When I got to the Rayburn House Office Building after school, Senator Something smelled cupcake. As I was clipping on his leash, he sniffed me all over, trying to figure out where I had hidden it.

"Stop it, Senator Something. I ate the cupcake."

That made him mad. He made me run with him all the way down to the bottom of Capitol Hill to the statue of General Grant. And then made me run back up again.

A bunch of reporters were standing around on a patch of dead grass called the House Triangle, where lawmakers went for a press conference when the Speaker wouldn't give them a press conference room. Senators had their own outside press conference spot called the Senate Swamp. I never saw any alligators there.

Since this was a Democratic press conference, it started late. Of course it did. Papa said 20 minutes late was called "Democratic Time." Back in the 20th century, Papa said President Clinton's press conferences started more than an hour late and they called it "Clinton Time."

Staffers kept checking their texts to see when their bosses were going to show up. The sound guy checked the microphone for the thousandth time. One reporter must have missed her lunch hour. She was sitting on the bench at the edge of the grass near the sidewalk, eating a sub sandwich.

"Let's go," Senator Something," I said. "We don't need to stand around waiting since we're not reporters."

He wasn't listening. He was frozen, his nose stuck up in the air. Senator Something had a really good nose.

"What is it, boy? Chickcharney?"

It wasn't Chickcharney. It was salami. Senator Something smelled his favorite food in the world.

Actually, every food in the world was Senator Something's favorite, but he particularly liked salami. When Senator Something got something into his head – or into his nose – that was it. He dragged me straight through the pack of reporters, over to the bench. Senator Something stopped right in front of the reporter.

"Well, hello there," said the girl.

Senator Something didn't whine. He didn't beg. He didn't even lick his lips. He just looked at the sandwich and looked at the reporter and made the saddest eyes.

"Oh, you sweet thing," she said and scratched his head and pulled on his ears.

Senator Something sighed deeply.

"He wants your salami," I said.

"Nonsense," said the reporter. "He just wants a little love." She patted the dog again. Senator Something made an even sadder face.

"Salami," I said.

She pulled a slice out of her sandwich and tore off a bit. "Is it all right if I give him a bite?"

"Well..." I said, but it was too late. Senator Something snarfed up the meat and sat back on his haunches, licking his lips.

The reporter laughed. "Your dog?"

"No. He belongs to Congresswoman Mitchell. I walk him for her. It's my job."

"Vicki Pearson. *Roll Call*. Nice to meet you."

Roll Call was the name of one of the Capitol Hill newspapers.

"Fina Mendoza, professional dog walker and detective."

"Detective!" she said. "What do you detect?"

"Lots of stuff." I knew from Papa not to tell reporters too much information.

"He's a very sweet dog," she said.

Members of Congress started lining up behind the microphone, trying to figure out who was going to talk first.

"Oops, back to work," she said. "Bye, Senator Something."

I noticed Papa standing near the other lawmakers. He was talking to Claudia. I pulled Senator Something back behind the TV cameras so that Papa wouldn't see us.

"This afternoon," said one of the lawmakers, stepping up to the microphone, "I am pleased to announce the creation of a bipartisan immigration team we're calling The Gang of Eight."

I knew bipartisan meant both Democrats and Republicans, but I didn't know there was a gang in Congress.

"Let me introduce one of those members, the man who delivered the Spanish language State of the Union response, Congressman Arturo Mendoza from California's 34th congressional district."

There was some applause, but just from the staffers. Reporters don't applaud.

Papa talked about "bipartisan cooperation" and "the most important challenge of our day" and on and on and on. Senator Something must have been bored, too. He started nosing his way toward the spot where Vicki was standing. I tried to pull him back, but it was no good. Reporters got bumped left and right, saying "hey!" and "watch it!" as Senator Something pushed his way to the front.

Vicki didn't notice. She was getting ready to ask a question as soon as the millionth lawmaker in a row finished his speech. Senator Something stopped right next to her, sticking his nose into her handbag.

"Congressman," she said, waving her hand in the air, "since the president said amnesty was off the table, I wanted to know why – hey! What are you doing?"

The members of Congress thought she was asking what they were doing about immigration, but she was talking to the dog. Senator Something had found the rest of her sandwich. He pulled it out of her bag and threw it down on the ground, tearing it apart to get at the salami. He shredded the paper wrapping. Lettuce and tomato flew this way and that. "Hey!" said one reporter as mustard landed on his jacket.

"Stop it, Senator Something!" I said as quietly as I could. "Stop it right now."

Papa saw it all. He opened his mouth to say something, but Claudia whispered in his ear and hurried around to the back side of the House Tri-angle, behind all the reporters. She pulled Senator Something's squeaky toy out of her purse. It was the little model of the Washington Monument, Senator Something's favorite. I must have left it in Papa's office.

Claudia squeaked it, then waved it in the air above the reporters' heads. Senator Something looked up, saw the toy, and dragged me away from the trashed sandwich toward Claudia. Claudia kept backing up, farther and farther away from the press conference, farther and farther away from Papa's not very happy face.

It was too late. Senator Something and I were both in the doghouse now.

At dinner that night, Papa didn't say anything about me and Senator Something crashing his press conference. Probably because Gabby was in full crabby mode.

"It's a dance. A school dance. It's not that big a deal."

"And your problem, mija?" asked Papa.

Gabby glared at Abuelita. Abuelita said nothing. She put the bowl of posole on the table with a thump. As soon as she left the room, Gabby continued. "Abuelita thinks she should be one of the chaperones. Abuelita!"

"Are you embarrassed by your grandmother?" asked Papa.

"Of course I am! Not all the time. Just when I'm going to my very first dance at my new school. I don't want everyone to think I'm some kind of space alien."

So I wasn't the only one who wanted a little less Abuelita in her life.

Abuelita brought in the salad.

"It is not a problem, Arturo," she said to Papa. "If Gabby doesn't want me there, I won't go. Simple as that."

She sat down and grabbed my left hand and Gabby's right hand. "May the Lord make us thankful for this food and this family..."

I could feel her squeezing my hand. Hard. I bet she was squeezing Gabby's hand even harder.

"And bless those not fortunate enough to have food and family," she said.

"A-MEN," said Gabby, grabbing her hand back and staring at Abuelita.

Ever since she came to Washington, Abuelita had a lot of ideas about what Gabby and I should be allowed to do. She didn't even like the idea of me walking Senator Something after school.

"You have homework, mija," she told me at dinner one night.

"I can do it, Abuelita. And my dog needs me! Congress needs me!"

"Leave her be, Mama," said Papa that night.

Papa thought he was in charge, but the truth was that Abuelita was the boss. Even the boss of

Papa. The time he asked her about making chile rellenos for dinner, Abuelita shook her head. "Oh, mijo, your middle has grown since you left California. Not enough lettuce and oranges. No fried foods for you."

"But ..." he protested.

"Do you want people to point at you on C-SPAN and say, 'there he is, the fat congressman'?"

Papa knew when to give up. He stopped asking for Abuelita's chile rellenos.

Abuelita had lots of opinions. She told Gabby to stop wearing what she called "street clothes" to school on casual Friday.

"But Abuelita, it's the one day a month when I don't have to wear that stupid uniform!" whined Gabby. "What about freedom of expression? It's my constitutional right!"

"You can express yourself in some way other than wearing a hoodie and leggings to school," she said. "You must show respect for your teachers."

Abuelita came up with a list of rules about what Gabby could and could not wear out of the house.

- No fake eyelashes. Even though all the ladies on the Hallmark Channel had layers and layers of lashes, Abuelita said they looked fake and fake lashes told people you were fake, too.

- Sensible shoes. In other words, no shoes that you couldn't walk a mile in when you were wearing them.
- No clothes that you could see through, even if you were wearing a tank top underneath.
- No blue hair. Or orange hair. Or green hair.
- No belly buttons showing.

I don't remember Abuelita squawking at us all the time when we lived in California. It was as if Washington, D.C. had turned our grandmother into an angry bird.

We were almost done eating, but Gabby and Abuelita were still mad about the dance. I tried to change the subject. "Papa, tell Abuelita about your Gang of Eight."

"What's this, Arturo? You are joining a gang?"

Papa had just put a big tomato into his mouth.

"It's not a real gang, Abuelita," I told her. "It's just a bunch of senators and congressmen fighting about immigration."

"Not fighting, mija," said Papa, swallowing. "Not exactly. It's been a long, long time since Congress has thought about what to do about all the people who have come to this country to make a better life. Should we send them back? If so, who should we send back? Who should we allow to stay?"

"Great," said Gabby, reaching for the bottle of salad dressing. "Another bunch of meetings. Maybe we'll see you sometime before Easter."

"Gabby, please do not grab across the table. Ask if you want something passed to you," said Abuelita.

Gabby rolled her eyes. "And why you, Papa?"

"Claudia says it's because Papa was so good on TV after the State of the Union," I said. "He was good at the press conference today, too."

Oops. Why did I bring that up? Now Papa was going to yell at me about bringing Senator Something to the House Triangle and almost ruining his press conference.

Papa didn't get a chance to yell at me. Abuelita had her own plans for Papa's new job. "Perfecto, Tutu," she said, clapping her hands. "Now you can fix everything, the way that President Reagan fixed everything so that I could become an American citizen."

Abuelita was born in Mexico. She came to this country to join our grandfather, working at a balloon factory and a car wash, getting paid in cash. She could never complain if her pay was less than what she had earned. She was afraid that her boss would report her to "la migra," the immigration police. Abuelita always said that President Ronald Reagan had changed her life.

"I had to pass the test," she said, "and I had to bring a wheelbarrow full of paper to prove that I had worked here and paid all of my taxes and never took any money from the government and never got into trouble with the law."

Gabby sighed. "You've told us this story a hundred times, Abuelita."

"It is the most important story of my life, mija," she said. "And now your father has the chance of a lifetime to help other immigrants. I'm proud of you, Tutu."

Chapter Eight

It rained all day Saturday, cold and dark and miserable. Gabby didn't care. She acted like it was the best day on planet Earth. Papa had persuaded Abuelita that there would be plenty of chaperones at Gabby's dance.

Gabby stared at herself in the mirror, then turned to me. "What do you think? Hair up or down?"

Gabby was asking *my* opinion?

"I think I look older with it up," she said, pulling her hair up into a scrunchie and twisting it around to make a bun.

I shrugged my shoulders. She still looked like Gabby to me. Except with purple fingernails.

"What are you going to wear?"

"It's a surprise," said Gabby. "My friend Olivia from band let me borrow one of her dresses. Want to watch me make smoky eyes?"

"No thanks." I didn't want to watch Gabby play with makeup. And since the weather was nasty, I would spend the afternoon doing research. "You don't need the laptop, right?"

"It's all yours," she said. "Still doing eagle research?"

"Sort of."

"Check out the Audubon Society," she said. "They're the bird people." Then she turned her music up way too loud, Gabby's way of telling me to get out of her room.

I shut my bedroom door and opened the laptop. I didn't know how to spell Audubon, but Google figured it out.

The website said Audubon was a guy who painted bird pictures. The Audubon Society protected birds and the places where they lived.

The website had a story about 13 bird superstitions. In other words, stories that weren't guaranteed to be true. I read them anyway. After all, the Demon Cat of Capitol Hill was supposed to be a myth, too, but then I met the actual cat. She wasn't as scary as she was in the stories.

Number one on the Audubon list: if a bird pooped on your head, it was supposed to be good luck. That should be good news for the president, even if he didn't think so.

There were a lot of other bird myths that were interesting. For example, when a swan bent its neck back over its body, it meant that a storm was coming. And if you went swimming and didn't want to drown, you were supposed to make sure there was a wren nearby. There was nothing about a Chick-charney.

The last myth on the list said that when a bird flew into a house, you should expect an important message. The same thing Monica said about Chick-charney! But maybe that message wasn't for Monica. Or even for me. Maybe it was for the president. I wondered what it was. I wrote down all the myths in my case book.

"Dinner, mijas!" called Abuelita from downstairs.

I looked at the clock. The afternoon had disappeared. I wondered whether Gabby was finished getting all dressed up for her dance. I tapped on her door.

"What?"

"Can I see?" I asked.

Gabby opened the door. Her hair was all fancy and she must have painted eight layers of mascara on her lashes. She was still in her bathrobe.

"Where's your dress?"

"I don't want to get spaghetti sauce all over it. C'mon. Let's eat."

I never did see the dress. It was still raining outside, and Gabby was wrapped up in a raincoat, her dancing shoes in her hand to keep them dry.

"But I want a picture, mija!" said Abuelita. "To send to your tías back in Los Angeles."

"I'm late, Abuelita!" she said, slamming the front door and dashing down the iron steps to her friend's parent's car.

"Teenagers," grumbled Abuelita. She was in a rainy mood herself.

Chapter Nine

It was a good thing that Senator Something really liked cold weather, since there was a lot of it in Washington in February. His orange fur was really thick and really long and he didn't mind getting his feet wet or cold. The grass was still damp from all the rain over the weekend, but at least today the sun started peeking through the clouds. It felt good to walk with the sun on your head. I think Senator Something felt that way, too.

Walking was good for detecting. Sometimes your brain worked better when you were moving around instead of sitting in front of a computer. Sometimes, the solution to a puzzle would drop from the sky and land right inside your head.

That was what happened. As we walked past the concrete fountains with no water in them this time of year, a thought fell out of the sky: maybe Monica was right. Maybe the entire Capitol police force had been barking up the wrong tree. They had been looking for the wrong kind of bird.

I thought about the pictures I'd seen online of Chickcharney. He looked like a scary owl with really, really long legs.

An owl! Maybe the mysterious bird in the Capitol was an owl. "What do you think, Senator Something?"

He barked in agreement.

"Do you think there are any owls with really long legs?"

Senator Something thought about this question, then looked up at me. He didn't seem to know. I had more research to do.

There was another dog running around the park over the parking garage. He was small with wiry fur and had a little bark that sounded like a squeak toy. He started yapping at Senator Something. Senator Something did not bark back. He just looked at me, kind of confused. Senator Something couldn't figure out why this little guy was so mad at him.

"Sorry about that," said a tall, bald man walking the tiny dog. "Saint Sebastian thinks he's the king of Capitol Hill."

"He doesn't act too saintly," I said, pulling hard on Senator Something's leash. I didn't want to get between the little king and Senator Something.

"Saint Sebastian," I said. "Was he a famous saint?"

"Not too famous. But he was a tough little guy," said the man. "Like this little guy." The mini dog knew that the man was talking about him. He wagged his mini tail and danced on his mini hind legs.

"Sebastian was a Roman guard. But he was also a Christian. When the Romans found out, they shot him with arrows."

"Did he die?"

"Eventually. He's the patron saint of archers, athletes, and soldiers."

That made more sense than all the things St. Valentine was in charge of.

He stuck out his hand. "Father Andrew."

"Fina Mendoza," I said, shaking his hand firmly. Papa said a strong handshake was important in Washington. I looked closely at his puffy jacket and sneakers. "You don't look like a priest."

"My collar's in the laundry."

"Really?"

"No. Just joking," he said.

"Priests get to have dogs?"

"Priests take the vow of obedience, poverty and such. No vow about dogs. My last pastor hated them. He must have been bit by some pooch when he was a kid. I had to wait until I got my new job before I could adopt Saint Sebastian."

The priest looked familiar. I tried to imagine him in his priest uniform. "Wait a minute," I said. "I know who you are. You're the House Chaplain."

"Guilty as charged. No arrows, please."

"You say the prayer before the lawmakers start arguing about stuff," I said.

"You must watch a lot of C-SPAN," he said.

"Only when I have to. They have it on the office TV all the time. My father is Congressman Arturo Mendoza. From California."

"Of course," he said.

"So what do you do after you say your prayer on the House floor?"

"Play a little golf, have a picnic at the Franciscan Monastery, grab a beer at Tortilla Coast."

"Really?"

"I wish," he said. "No, the House Chaplain is a full-time job. There are lots of tough issues for lawmakers. I'm there to listen. And to advise."

Saint Sebastian had stopped barking. Now he was sniffing all over Senator Something, who decided he was the bigger dog and ignored him.

"This is Senator Something," I said. "One of my clients."

"Clients!"

"I walk dogs after school. It's my job," I said.

"Well, Fina Mendoza, do you ever take on new clients? Sometimes I have to hear confessions or preside at a funeral or advise a lawmaker. But the good Saint still needs a walk. Interested?"

"I charge five dollars a day," I said, wondering whether a priest had that kind of money.

"Sounds reasonable," he said.

"And I have to get Papa and Abuelita's permission."

"Again, reasonable."

"And Senator Something has to approve," I said.

Father Andrew leaned over to go nose to nose with Senator Something. "What do you say, Senator?"

The shaggy orange tail wagged like crazy. Senator Something liked the tall priest, but I could tell he wasn't so sure about the little dog. Father Andrew didn't notice.

"Looks like we have a deal," he said.

We shook hands again. Everybody shook hands in Washington.

Walking two dogs at the same time wasn't as easy as I thought it would be.

With Senator Something, we would have a serious discussion before we left the office about what we were going to do on our walks. If I told him I had a lot of homework to do and didn't have time to take him all the way down the hill to the Bartholdi Fountain, I'd promise to do it another day. I would also promise to give him a doggie treat if he agreed to come back to the office without a fuss. It worked most of the time. I felt like a dog walking expert.

Walking Saint Sebastian was totally different. He was like a little kid. He had his own way of getting what he wanted, when he wanted it. When Saint Sebastian got an idea into his head about something, he would turn around and look at me and whine. A loud, squeaky whine. It was so loud that strangers on the street would look at me like I was torturing him or something.

Saint Sebastian also loved garbage cans, smelling every little thing around the outside, and rolling in the stinky fast food wrappers and cigarettes that didn't make it inside the can. Father Andrew was not very happy when his dog came back to the office smelling like an ashtray. Saint Sebastian was certainly no saint.

When I tried to walk Saint Sebastian with Senator Something, they both wanted to be in charge. One dog wanted to go one way and the other one wanted to go the other way, both pulling on their leashes. I thought my arms were going to come off.

When I finally got the two dogs to go in the same direction, Saint Sebastian would duck under the leash of Senator Something and then walk around in front of him until the two leashes were completely tangled up. I tripped, scraping my knee and putting a hole in my tights.

Senator Something wasn't acting very saintly, either. He knew his legs were about ten times as long as Saint Sebastian's, and he made it a point to take the longest steps possible. That didn't stop Saint Sebastian. For a dog with such little feet, Saint Sebastian moved just as fast as Senator Something.

I wasn't lying when I told Papa I was getting lots of exercise walking dogs.

The worst part was that Senator Something knew he was being mean. He kept looking back at the scruffy little dog with a sneer on his face, as if to say, "some king of Capitol Hill you are."

Walking two dogs took a lot more time than walking one. It was time I wasn't spending looking for Chickcharney. Tomorrow, I promised myself, tomorrow I would make time to look for Chickcharney. I had to find him for Monica. I had to hear his message.

Even if it wasn't for me.

Chapter Ten

Papa was on TV tonight. It was one of those politics shows where you see the people in boxes. Papa's box was on the left. The interviewer asked why the Gang of Eight was still meeting since no progress seemed to be happening.

"We've been having very good discussions," said Papa.

"But no proposals," said the TV lady.

"Not yet," said Papa.

I was already in my pajamas by the time Papa came home. He seemed sad when he tucked me in, and I wanted to say something nice.

"You looked good on TV tonight, Papa. Not so orange."

He laughed and kissed me on the forehead.

"Twenty minutes of reading and then lights out. Good night, mija."

"G'night, Papa."

I almost told Papa about my new investigation. But if I told him that I wanted to find Chickcharney because the bird had a message from Mama, he might not believe me. And if he did believe me, it would make him sad that the bird had a message for me but not for him.

I would continue my investigation by myself. I flipped through the library book's pages and pages of bird pictures. It divided the birds into groups like gulls or warblers or loons. I found the owl family.

I knew there were owls in Washington, D.C. You could hear them around Halloween, hoot hooting at night. But the owls in the book just looked like regular owls. Barn Owls with heart-shaped faces, Great Horned Owls with eyebrows that poked up into feathered spikes on top of their heads, Snowy Owls that looked like yellow-eyed snowmen. None of them looked like Chickcharney.

The baby owls were the spookiest. Their skinny bodies and huge black eyes made them look like space aliens.

I was about to give up. And then I turned the page. There he was! Chickcharney!

His official name was Athene cunicularia, named after the Greek goddess Athena. In Spanish, Mochuelo de Madriguera: a Burrowing Owl. He wasn't very big, only about nine inches tall. He had spots, with a round head, and really long legs. He lived in open farmland, golf courses, and airports. He built his nest underground.

The Zuni tribe called Burrowing Owls the "priest of the prairie dogs" because a wise old owl once saved a village of prairie dogs from flooding. The owl got a beetle to eat a bunch of beans, and then collected its farts to blow away the rain clouds. Now that was a weird legend.

The book said Burrowing Owls didn't eat beans, but they did eat dragonflies and lizards and even baby rabbits. And mice. If there was one thing I learned from my first case investigating the Demon Cat of Capitol Hill, it was that the U.S. Capitol had lots of mice. If Monica forgot to put out leftovers for her Chickcharney, at least it would have plenty to eat.

All of that information was interesting, but there was one problem: there weren't any Burrowing Owls in Washington D.C. Most of them lived in Mexico or Florida or states out west where it was hot most of the time. If a Californian like me felt cold here in February, even when I was wearing a hat, gloves, and my new coat, what chance did a Burrowing Owl have?

The book said it was rare to see a Burrowing Owl, even out west, because the population was shrinking. Probably because a golf course was a dangerous place for a bird to live with golf balls flying and golf carts racing all over the place. It wasn't very likely that Burrowing Owls were flying around Washington. But at least I could show Monica a picture of one and see if I was on the right track.

There was nothing in the book about Burrowing Owls being called Chickcharneys, and nothing about them delivering secret messages.

There was a shriek downstairs that definitely did not sound like a bird. It was Gabby.

"Unbelievable!" she shouted. "Fina come see!"

I ran downstairs. Gabby was practically dancing in front of the TV. So was the weather guy as he pointed to the weather map.

"It's a blizzard," he said. "Coming our way. A big one! Jaw dropping! Amazing amounts of snow expected. The storm of the century!"

"Finally, Fina. Looks like you're going to get your wish. A real snowstorm," said Gabby.

"Yes!" I said, raising a fist in the air.

The weather guy waved his arms wildly. "Another Snowmageddon," he said. "Snoverkill! Snowpocalypse! Snowmazilla!"

I thought the names were pretty funny. Gabby and I started making up some of our own. Snow White-Out. Frozen 3. Game of Snow.

A bunch of sentences in orange letters moved across the bottom of the screen. "All schools in the District of Columbia, Maryland, and Virginia will be closed tomorrow. Metro will run limited service. All government buildings will be shut down."

"No school!" we screamed at the same time.

Abuelita clucked and went into the kitchen.

I started thinking. "I wonder how you get ready for a snowstorm? Do you put together a snowstorm kit? Like an earthquake kit? You know, toilet paper, water for three days, first aid stuff..."

Gabby nodded. "Flashlights and batteries," she said. "Just in case the lights go out."

I could hear Abuelita banging pots and pans around on the stove.

"What is going on down here?" asked Papa, marching down the stairs. "I can't hear myself think."

Gabby and I pointed to the kitchen.

"Mama? Que pasa?"

"Preparing for Snowmazilla," she called from the other room.

"Papa, the weather guy says it's a ginormous storm! The entire city is shutting down!"

"I know. They're shutting down Congress tomorrow."

I looked out the window. No snow. At least, not yet.

"What do we do, Papa?" I asked.

Papa was a Californian like me and Gabby and Abuelita, but he had lived in Washington for a couple of winters. He knew about snowstorms. "Knowing D.C. weather," he said, "It will probably turn out to be a whole lot of nothing. But just in case..."

Just in case meant we spent an hour finding the snow shovels and our boots and extra hats and gloves. Abuelita cooked up enough of the beef stew she called birria de res to feed all of Capitol Hill. Gabby rounded up all of the batteries in the house, and we charged up the laptop and all of Papa's phones. We charged up Gabby and Abuelita's phones, too.

Eventually, we ran out of things to charge up, so we sat in front of the TV and watched the purple wave on the weather map slowly moving over Washington, D.C.

"Go to bed," said Papa. "It won't start snowing really hard until after midnight."

So we went to bed. But it was like Christmas Eve, when you could hardly keep your eyes shut, waiting for something exciting to happen.

Chapter Eleven

When I woke up, everything was really quiet, as if the street was cushioned in cotton. It looked like cotton, too. It had snowed a little bit before Christmas, what Papa called "a dusting," but this was real, thick, perfect snow. The kind of snow you saw in movies. It covered the little patch of front lawn, the sidewalks, the streets, everything. The tree branches were thick with white. So were the cars parked on our street. The street itself disappeared under a blanket of snow. And it kept falling.

I knew that Trina, my best friend back in L.A., would be jealous. She wanted to come visit me in D.C. just to see snow falling from the sky. I grabbed the family phone and texted Trina a video of snow falling. She texted me back a sad face emoji and a snowman.

I pulled on my tights and a tee shirt and another tee shirt and a sweater tunic and my fleeciest leggings and two pairs of socks. I pulled on my boots and grabbed my jacket. I stuck my hands into thick gloves. I was ready.

Except that I had to go to the bathroom, which meant taking off half the clothes I'd just spent ten minutes putting on. Getting ready for snow meant a lot of putting clothes on and taking them off.

I decided that Gabby wouldn't want to be sleeping away our first snowstorm, so I pounded on her door.

"Go away," she moaned.

"Gabby! Look out the window."

Five minutes later, she was dressed in a million sweaters and racing me to the front door. We tramped around outside, slushing our way through thick snow. Our boots sunk down into the white mush. Even with all those layers of clothing, my nose was still cold. Not freezing cold. More like my nose was saying, "Hey, what about me?"

"Heads up!" Gabby shouted as a snowball just missed my head.

The battle was on. We threw handful after handful of snow at each other until we were both covered in melting flakes. We even made a little snowman, dressing him in Abuelita's knitted hat and the scarf Gabby gave me for Christmas. The scarf was a joke. Gabby knew I hated scarves, even when it was really cold, but she wrapped one up anyway as a present for me under the tree. The scarf looked better on the snowman.

"What do you want to do now?" asked Gabby.

Papa stuck his head out the front door. "Bored already? Make yourselves useful."

He held up two shovels and nodded at the walkway in front of our house, buried in white. "You and Gabby can get it done in half an hour."

"Why do we have to do it?" asked Gabby.

"Do you want your grandmother to slip and fall? Shoveling the sidewalk is the price we pay for living in a place with snow."

Papa went back inside. Gabby and I looked at each other.

"I don't know how to shovel snow," I said.

"You just stick the shovel in and dig."

I watched Gabby work for a minute or two and then picked up my shovel.

"Race you," she said. "You start shoveling from the sidewalk and I'll start from here. Whoever gets to the rose bush first wins."

"I don't want to race –"

"On your mark, get set, go!" shouted Gabby.

She started shoveling like Mike Mulligan's steam shovel. I stuck the shovel in deeper. It got stuck. I pulled it out and fell backwards, landing on my butt. Gabby rolled her eyes. I tried again, taking a smaller scoop of snow and dumping it on what used to be the lawn. That wasn't so hard. I took another shovel full. And another. It was like Abuelita's joke about how you eat an elephant: take little bites. Taking little bites of snow was easy. Soon I was moving as fast as Gabby.

We were both getting close to the rose bush – or at least what was probably a rose bush since we'd never seen it actually bloom with roses.

"I'm going to win!" said Gabby.

"Not a chance!" I said.

We met in the middle, both of us clearing the sidewalk in front of the rose bush at exactly the same time.

"Tie!" we said together, and laughed. We touched shovels.

"The California girls can show these D.C. folks how it's done," said Gabby.

I could smell the cinnamon from the hot chocolate as soon as I opened the front door.

"Boots off!" said Abuelita. "And jackets and scarves and hats and gloves. All of it."

That was the other thing about snow. It melted. Abuelita held out a laundry basket for our clothes and handed each of us a towel. We were pretty wet. "Upstairs to change," she said. "Then a nice hot cup of cocoa."

The rest of the day was pretty boring. Papa built a fire in the fireplace and then went upstairs to make some phone calls. Gabby went down to the basement to practice her clarinet. Abuelita worked on a jigsaw puzzle at the dining room table.

The second day was even more boring.

Trina texted me, begging for more pictures of snow. I sent her the shot of our sad snowman, but I also told her the truth: snow was really, really fun when it fell from the sky, and when there was enough of it for school to call a snow day and we got to stay home. It wasn't so much fun when it melted during the late afternoon and froze up again at night, turning the sidewalks into ice skating rinks without the skates. I fell two times and had the bruises to prove it.

It wasn't fun when the snowplow scooped up all the snow and half the gravel on the street, and dumped it on the curb in a giant dirty brown frozen pile. It definitely wasn't fun to watch the neighborhood dogs turn the snow yellow.

Flakes started falling again at lunch time. I watched from the window for a while. The snow was covering up all the shoveling Gabby and I had done. I wasn't looking forward to starting all over again.

I grabbed the laptop and camped out on the couch. At least I could do some detecting work. I googled Burrowing Owls and then I googled Chickcharney and looked at the pictures side by side. Long legs, check. Owlish face, check. A Burrowing Owl didn't have scary looking hands like Chickcharney. Or the lizard tail. But Chickcharney *had* to be a Burrowing Owl.

Then I remembered Senator Something's warning about jumping to conclusions. Maybe there was another explanation.

I tried to remember what the bird sounded like. I found a webpage from Cornell University with sound recordings from all kinds of Burrowing Owls. The Florida owl's tweet added a hoot at the end. Definitely not the sound I heard. I clicked on another button. This time, the Burrowing Owl made a tweet that sounded like a Blue Jay.

Maybe I had jumped to conclusions. Maybe the bird wasn't a Burrowing Owl after all. And how could a Burrowing Owl get to Washington, D.C.? Did it get caught in a tornado, pushed across the country? Maybe it was somebody's pet, though the only person I could think of who had a pet owl was Harry Potter. Think. Who would have a Burrowing Owl in Washington, D.C.? And then I thought of exactly the place: the National Zoo! Maybe they had a Burrowing Owl!

I grabbed the family phone and called the zoo. I got a recording. "The Smithsonian National Zoo is temporarily closed due to the snow emergency. For more information, please visit our website…"

Right. I forgot. Everything was closed because of Snowmazilla. I clicked on the website and looked at the list of animals. Boa constrictor, bobcat, brown pelican… There it was! The National Zoo had a pair of Burrowing Owls!

But why would an owl from the National Zoo end up in the U.S. Capitol? Unless it escaped.

I did some more googling. I read that Ollie the bobcat escaped from the National Zoo, but they found him two days later, hanging around the bird house looking for lunch. Another time, a red panda named Rusty escaped from the zoo and ended up in a neighborhood a few miles away. In Kansas, a flamingo escaped and nobody found him for eight years! Why couldn't a Burrowing Owl escape from the National Zoo and end up in the U.S. Capitol?

I would have to wait until Snowmazilla was over and I could talk to the zookeepers.

I had run out of things to do. I finished reading "Garvey's Choice" and two other books that I brought home from the library. I even cleaned my room.

I checked out the Eagle Cam. Snow was falling on the trees and the nest. Both of the eagles were there, sitting practically on top of each other, trying to keep warm. Mr. President stood up and stretched. He shook off the ice that had crusted onto his wings and huddled back down.

Was Monica's Chickcharney warm tonight? Was there ice on his wings as well?

We were stuck at home for three whole days. We ran out of things to watch on Netflix and couldn't find the dice for the Monopoly set. Papa made Gabby practice her clarinet twice a day now. You could tell she wasn't happy about it. Her music sounded more like crow caws. Everybody was getting on everybody else's nerves. Especially Abuelita.

It started when Gabby drank the last cup of coffee. That was new: Gabby drinking coffee. Abuelita would "tut tut" but nobody stopped her.

"She's nearly sixteen now," Papa told Abuelita. "She can make decisions for herself about drinking coffee."

Abuelita picked up the empty coffee pot. "If a person is grown up enough to drink coffee, they are also grown up enough to make a fresh pot."

"I'm tired of being treated like a baby," whispered Gabby.

"How do you think I feel?" I said.

"Yeah, but you <u>are</u> a baby."

"Double digits!"

Gabby ignored this. She'd been double digits for years.

"Gabby," said Abuelita, shaking the glass pot.

"There isn't anymore," whined Gabby, kicking the table leg. "We're out of coffee."

"Then you can walk yourself up to the market and get some."

Abuelita put the glass pot on the table in front of Gabby.

"Nothing's open!" said Gabby, waving her hand. Which hit the pot. Which went crashing to the floor, smashing into a dozen pieces.

"Now you've done it, miss!" said Abuelita.

"I didn't do anything," said Gabby as she stormed upstairs.

"Mama, it was an accident," said Papa.

"Don't you start with me, Arturo!" she said and marched downstairs to the basement.

We weren't the only ones with nothing to do. All of Washington had shut down. The internet had pictures of people snowshoeing on the National Mall. A giant snowball fight broke out in Dupont Circle with about a hundred strangers hitting each other with chunks of snow. A bunch of kids brought their sleds to Capitol Hill, but the Capitol police wouldn't let them slide down.

By the third day of Snowmazilla, even the weather guy sounded tired of snow. Tonight, he reported that more than two feet had fallen on Washington during the storm. It was so heavy in some places, power lines had been knocked down and half the city lost electricity. He showed a satellite picture of Washington, D.C. from space. It was all white.

It was funny, though. All of the stories on the news were about Snowmazilla. All of them. The story about the bird that pooped on the president had disappeared completely. There were no more stories in *The Washington Post*, nothing on the TV or on WTOP, the radio news station. I asked Papa why.

"The news cycle has moved on," he said.

"News cycle?" I pictured a giant bicycle made out of newspapers riding off through the snow.

"Snowmazilla is the news of the day," he said. "Reporters have completely forgotten about that bird."

I wondered if the president had forgotten about the bird. Maybe he was happy that people were talking about something else. Did Snowmazilla also mean the Capitol police and the Secret Service had also stopped looking for the bird?

Monica wouldn't have forgotten. She would still be worried about Chickcharney. I knew my job was not yet done.

Chapter Twelve

Finally, we were going back to school. I missed Michael and Ms. Greenwood. I even missed math class.

The sun was out and already a lot of the snow was melting. Patches of dead grass appeared in our tiny front yard. There were tall piles where the plows had pushed the dirty snow onto the curbs. Not everybody in the neighborhood had shoveled their sidewalk. Some of the snow melted and froze again overnight. That turned it into ice, so walking to school was slippery.

At recess, everybody wanted to tell their Snowmazilla story. Everybody but Becka. She didn't have a snow story. She wasn't even in Washington when the storm hit.

"The minute my mother saw that snowstorm heading to D.C., she put us on a plane. It was so much nicer to be at the beach," she said. "Florida is so beautiful this time of year."

Nobody cared about Becka or Florida or the beach. They only wanted to talk about their snow adventures. Inside the classroom, it was hard to concentrate on the rules of punctuation. Ms. Greenwood sighed and tried something else.

"Let's turn to science."

The class groaned.

"Can anyone explain why so much snow fell in Washington?" she asked.

Hands waved in the air. Everyone had been watching the weather guys. Everyone was an expert. The afternoon sped by with explanations of Doppler Radar and how to read a weather map and what a high pressure system over Canada meant to us way down here in Washington. I was surprised when I heard the bell for the end of school.

I was looking forward to seeing Senator Something and Saint Sebastian again, but I wasn't looking forward to walking them together. I had to find a way to walk two dogs without getting all tangled up in the leashes. For now, I figured the best way was to walk them separately.

It was the perfect day to try out my solution since Senator Something was getting a haircut this afternoon. I guess when you had all that long, orange hair, you needed a haircut every few weeks.

So it was just Saint Sebastian and me. I picked him up at the House Chaplain's office inside the Capitol. It was down some steep stairs near the Crypt.

Saint Sebastian was asleep in his doggie bed, a purple fleecy square in the corner. Father Andrew handed me the leash.

"Careful. Don't lose him in the piles of snow," he said.

I decided we'd walk on the Senate side of the Capitol where the snow had melted and there were more trees than garbage cans.

Of course, Saint Sebastian wanted to smell each and every tree. It took a while. There were a lot of trees.

Then he stopped, frozen like a statue. I could see his tiny nose twitching. He seemed to point his foot at a branch high up in the tree, posing like a ballet dancer, not moving.

I looked up. Sitting on the bare branch was a black bird with a red patch on its shoulder. The bird tipped its head to look at us. Saint Sebastian looked right back. Then the bird spread its wings and took off, circling overhead a couple of times, as if to say, "I'm not scared of an itty bitty dog like you!"

Saint Sebastian unfroze from his pointing position, shook himself all over, and started marching away.

When I told Father Andrew what had happened, he just laughed. "They told me he was part bird dog when I got him from the pound."

"He doesn't look like a bird," I said.

"I don't know about that," said the priest. "His hair kind of sticks out like bird feathers." Saint Sebastian gave him a dirty look. Father Andrew scratched the dog's head to let him know that he didn't mean it. "A bird dog is the kind of breed that hunters use to find ducks and quail. I think you've discovered his secret identity."

I liked the idea that Saint Sebastian was an undercover dog. Maybe he had other secret identities, too. Maybe he spoke some foreign language or could climb up the side of a building. Maybe the CIA had trained him as a special agent. Or maybe he was just a plain old bird dog.

Bird dog. Bird dog! Saint Sebastian was exactly who I needed to help me track down Chickcharney.

"What do you think, boy?" I whispered in his ear. "Want to do some more bird hunting?"

Saint Sebastian put his ugly little face right next to mine and licked my cheek. I guess that meant yes.

I looked at the clock on Father Andrew's wall. Quarter to five.

"We'll start tomorrow, Saint Sebastian. I've got to make an important phone call."

I hurried back to Papa's office and borrowed the family phone.

"Smithsonian National Zoo," said a voice.

"Could you please connect me with the bird department?"

"I'm sorry," the lady said. "The bird house is closed."

"I thought you were open again now that Snowmazilla is over."

"We are open. The zoo, I mean. It's the bird house that's closed. For remodeling."

"Closed," I repeated.

"It was a very old building," she said. "But the new bird house will be better than ever."

I was sure it would be a wonderful new bird house. But I needed information now.

"What happens to the birds if the bird house is closed? Who takes care of them?"

"Just a minute, please. I have another call."

She put me on hold and I listened to some boring music for a long time. Finally, someone else picked up the phone. "Bird house."

"Are you missing a bird," I asked. "An owl? A Burrowing Owl?"

"May I ask who's calling?" asked the girl on the phone.

"My name is Fina Mendoza. I've found a Burrowing Owl in the basement of the U.S. Capitol. At least I think it's a Burrowing Owl. And I know Burrowing Owls don't live in Washington, D.C. except at the National Zoo, so I figured it was yours. Are you missing an owl?"

"I don't think so," said the girl on the phone. "I'm just an intern."

I knew all about interns. They were the college students who came to Washington to practice working for the government. A lot of them practiced by answering phones in the offices of lawmakers on Capitol Hill, or in this case, answering the phone in the zoo's bird department. Interns got dressed up in lady jackets like everybody else in Washington, but they really didn't know very much. In Papa's office, the interns were always asking Claudia how to answer the questions from people on the phone. This zoo intern didn't know much, either.

"Is there anyone there I could speak to?" I asked. "About a missing owl?"

"Why don't you leave your name and number and I'll have someone call you back in the morning," she said. I gave her the family phone's number and told her it was important.

Being a detective meant a lot of waiting around for people to call you back. I wasn't good at waiting around. I had other clues to investigate.

Chapter Thirteen

Who knew Abuelita had an Instagram account?

She said it was so that she could follow her favorite singer Pitbull, but she also followed Papa's official congressional Instagram account. And, apparently, Gabby's.

"Dios mio!" Abuelita shouted when she saw the picture. I peeked over her shoulder to look at the screen. It was a selfie of Gabby at her school dance. I recognized the purple fingernails. Gabby's hair was up, her eyes were plastered with mascara, and she was wearing a dress I'd never seen before, a dress held up by skinny little straps with a great big slash across the middle. You could see her belly button. A pierced belly button with a tiny gold ring.

When Gabby walked in the front door, she didn't even get a chance to put down her backpack.

"What is the meaning of this?" Abuelita demanded.

"What's the meaning of what?" asked Gabby.

I made a face, trying to warn her. Abuelita pointed to her phone.

"What kind of young woman puts a picture of her stomach on Instapost?"

"Instagram. It's just a dress," whined Gabby.

"Do all of your dresses show off your belly button? A belly button with an earring of its own?"

"It's a piercing, not an earring."

"And that phone of yours, sharing pictures of your naked stomach with the world. If you cannot use a phone in a responsible manner, you shouldn't be using it at all. No social media."

"But everybody's on social, Abuelita. That's how we talk to each other!" said Gabby.

"We?"

"People younger than a hundred and fifty."

"Why don't you just use your mouths? You are grounded."

"But tonight's the basketball game and ..."

"Starting right now. And hand over the phone."

Gabby stared at Abuelita. And then stared at me. "What are you looking at?"

"Nothing."

"Now, mija," said Abuelita, putting out her hand.

Gabby fished her phone out of her backpack and practically slammed it down on the coffee table.

Abuelita put the phone in her pocket. "And I'm calling your father."

Gabby ran upstairs. I heard her slam the door to her room.

Abuelita looked at me. "Unless you have homework, Fina, you can go fold laundry."

I did have homework, but decided it would be better to hang out with the sheets and towels.

I didn't understand why Gabby would want to show off her belly button in the middle of February. I always wore four layers whenever I left the house for school: undershirt, polo shirt, hoodie, and overcoat. It made me shiver just to think about naked skin in 30-degree weather.

I headed down to the basement. Our house was really old. Down here, you could hear things through the floor boards. I heard Abuelita calling Papa at the Capitol. I knew he was at another Gang of Eight meeting. Except it was only a Gang of Seven now. One of the congressmen got mad and quit.

It didn't take Papa very long to get home. "Gabby, what were you thinking?" It wasn't a question. Papa was mad.

"It's just a stupid picture," said Gabby.

"Stupid is right."

I could hear every word as I matched up socks, warm from the dryer.

"You aren't even ON Instagram," said Gabby. "You make Claudia post all your congressional pictures and stuff."

"And you think that makes it all right?"

I stayed downstairs for a long time. That night, I tapped on Gabby's door.

"Go away," she said.

"It's me, Gabby."

I heard her sigh, pad across the floor to unlock her bedroom door, stomp back, and flop on her bed. I poked my head inside to see if she'd throw a pillow at me. She didn't. I went in and shut the door. Gabby was sitting cross-legged on her bed, picking at the bits of purple nail polish still on her fingers.

"Why is she so mean to me?" she demanded, pounding the pillow with her fist.

"You're not the only one she's picking on," I said. "She tried to talk Papa into making me give up my dog walking job."

"That won't happen," said Gabby. "Congresswoman Mitchell likes you. And she's on that immigration gang with Papa. If Papa wants her to listen to any of his ideas, he doesn't want to make her mad by making her walk her own dog."

I hoped Gabby was right, but I wasn't sure.

"Abuelita never gets really mad at you the way she does at me," said Gabby.

"That's not true."

But maybe it was true. Gabby could make me crazy sometimes, but Gabby and Abuelita sometimes acted like they hated each other.

"She's always liked you better. I've heard her call you 'her favorite granddaughter' a million times."

"It's only because they gave me her same name," I said.

"Saint Josefina," she said in her snarkiest voice.

"It's not my fault!"

Now Gabby was mad at me. No, I thought. Not mad. Jealous. But what could Gabby be jealous about? She was the one who got to stay up past ten o'clock. She was the one who got to ride the Metro all by herself. She was the one with her own cell-phone.

"Sometimes I wish she'd stayed in California," said Gabby. "We were doing all right here in D.C. without her."

I thought about all the dinners Gabby had burned when she was in charge of cooking, compared to all the really good dinners Abuelita made. I kept my mouth shut.

"She wasn't like this back when we all lived in Los Angeles."

Gabby was right. Abuelita never acted like a prison guard back in California. What was different? For one thing, she was always busy in California. She was on a zillion committees at Sacred Heart, our church back in L.A. She wasn't on any church committees here. We didn't even have a church yet in D.C. Back in Los Angeles, our house was always full of familia, all of our cousins and aunts and uncles. The only family Abuelita had here in Washington was us.

"Maybe she's homesick," I said.

"For what?" asked Gabby. "All those bus trips to the Indian casino out near Palm Springs?"

"Maybe she's homesick for her friends on the bus."

Gabby thought about this for a minute. "You know, maybe you're right. Maybe she's just lonesome. She was always helping with the school bake sale or the church carnival. Remember the time she took first aid training and kept practicing on us? Maybe Abuelita just needs someone else to worry about. Other than us. I wish Mama was here. She'd know what to do."

"Don't you wish..." I said, and then stopped. Should I tell Gabby about the maybe message from Mama?

"Don't you wish," I started again, "that you could just check your voicemail and there'd be a message from Mama?"

Gabby smiled, but her smile drooped down at the corners of her mouth. "That would be something," she said in a remembering kind of voice.

"What do you think she would say?" I asked.

Gabby thought for a minute. "That she loves us. And to take care of Papa."

Should I tell Gabby about Chickcharney? About its message?

"Gabby, suppose I told you there might be a message from Mama waiting for us."

"Like some lost letter from the post office?"

"Sort of," I said. How could I explain that the message was coming from a mythical bird from the Caribbean?

"I'd love to see that letter," she sighed. "I know one thing. Mama wouldn't kick me off Instagram over a stupid dance dress."

I wasn't so sure about that.

Chapter Fourteen

Gabby was grounded like forever.

"Can I at least have my phone back?" she asked.

"As soon as you prove to me that you have some common sense," said Papa.

Papa had dark circles under his eyes. He went to meetings almost every night, but things weren't going very well. The Gang of Seven had shrunk to a Gang of Six. This time, one of the senators dropped out of the committee.

"Are you going to quit the Gang too, Papa?" I asked.

"Never give up, never give in," he said, quoting his favorite science fiction movie.

Abuelita decided it was time to pick a church.

When we first moved to Washington, Papa took us "church shopping." Every Sunday we would try out a new place to go to Mass. The problem was that none of the churches felt like home. After a while, we stopped looking. Not Abuelita.

On Saturday, Gabby begged me to get Abuelita out of the house. I decided to show Abuelita more of Washington. We walked down Capitol Hill toward the river and the baseball stadium. On the busiest part of South Capitol Street, she stopped suddenly in front of a sign. It read "Our Lady of Refuge." The church was ancient, built out of dirty gray stone with a square bell tower. Abuelita pointed to the rose in the stained glass window over the front door.

"It is for Our Lady," she said. "Remember the story of Our Lady of Guadalupe? Roses in winter. Mary sent Juan Diego back to the bishop with his cloak full of roses to prove that he really did see Our Lady and that she really did want a church built on that hill."

"And when he dropped his cloak," I said, "the roses fell to the floor. The bishop ignored the roses, but got all excited about the picture of Our Lady of Guadalupe on his cloak." I knew the story. We always celebrated Our Lady of Guadalupe day on December 12th at my old school.

"It is a sign," said Abuelita. "Tomorrow, we will all go to mass right here. No more church shopping."

On Sunday, Abuelita made all of us wear our church clothes and marched us down Capitol Hill to Our Lady of Refuge. Inside, it was kind of beat-up, with green carpet that looked like Astroturf and candles you could get at the dollar store. There was a crack under one of the stained glass windows and brown stains ran all the way down the wall.

"Water damage," mumbled Papa.

The bells were silent. A scrap of paper tied to the fence said the bell tower was cracked because of the earthquake they had in Washington a few years ago. The paper also told you where you could send money to help fix the tower. It was a lot of money.

We had earthquakes all the time in California. I was surprised that they had earthquakes here. Papa said everybody in Washington was surprised, too.

It was a protest-y kind of church. There were posters warning about climate change in the entryway. A huge barrel, half full of groceries for the food bank, sat near the back door. There was a sign-up sheet on the wall for volunteers to make sandwiches on Wednesdays to give to the homeless men and women who slept outside on the streets near the church.

There were only about fourteen people in the pews. With Papa, Abuelita, Gabby and me, that made eighteen. The old pipe organ groaned and then started to play a hymn I knew from California. "All are welcome," we sang.

One really loud voice came from the back of the church, singing louder than everyone else put together. He wasn't a very good singer. I turned around. It was Father Andrew. Saint Sebastian wasn't with him. I guess dogs don't have to go to church every Sunday. Even the dogs of priests.

Father Andrew marched up to the altar, singing even louder. In his sermon, he talked about what it meant to be a family – not just your father and grandmother and your sister Gabby, but the family of human beings. "What is our responsibility to our brothers and sisters who leave their home country to escape violence or poverty?" he asked. "Do we turn our backs?"

He was talking about immigration. I looked at Papa. He was listening, but he was looking down at the ugly carpet. He squirmed around in the pew. It was like me in class when I didn't want to be called on by Ms. Greenwood. But Father Andrew called on Papa anyway. Sort of.

"We are at a tipping point of history," he said. "Congress is at this very moment taking a look at immigration reform for the first time in a generation."

Papa slumped down in his seat. Father Andrew knew that Papa was one of the Gang of Eight. Or rather, the Gang of Six.

"Some have a seat at the table where we can change the laws of this great land," he said as his microphone crackled, "but what about the rest of us?"

Abuelita sat up straight as a tree. I thought about all the stories she told at the dinner table about coming to this country, how she ran through traffic to see the statue of Ronald Reagan, the president she worshipped because he helped her become a citizen.

"There are three things each one of us can do," he said. "We can pray for wisdom for our elected officials. We can make a phone call or write a letter to our member of Congress. And we can come to a meeting Tuesday night and talk about doing more."

"We're going," Abuelita whispered to me.

"But I have homework," I whispered back.

"Then I am going," she said. "Now shush."

When Papa and I came home Tuesday night from the Capitol, there was a note from Abuelita on the dining room table. "Gone to church," it said. "Dinner on the stove."

Papa thought that meant a prayer group, like the ones at our church in L.A. I knew it meant the immigration meeting Father Andrew talked about at mass.

Abuelita came home from the meeting in a car I didn't recognize. A woman in the backseat leaned out the window. "See you next week, Fina!" Only Abuelita's friends call her Fina. I wondered who these new friends were.

Abuelita was humming when she unlocked the front door and came inside. It was past my bedtime, but I stuck my head over the bannister at the top of the stairs. She was still humming as she took off her gloves and her scarf and her hat and her coat. She hummed some more as she pulled off her snow boots and stuck them in the hall closet.

"How was it, Abuelita?"

"It's late, mija, and you have school tomorrow. Back in bed."

"But who are those people?" I asked.

"I'll tell you all about it tomorrow when I walk you halfway to school," she said.

Rats. I hoped maybe she was out so late that she'd sleep in and let me walk to school by myself. No such luck. She was still walking me part way, every day, even though I begged her a hundred and one times to let me walk without her.

Abuelita didn't say much on the walk to school. She moved so fast I could hardly keep up. It was really cold. My nose felt frozen. I still wasn't wearing a scarf. I still thought scarves looked stupid.

"What did you do at that meeting, Abuelita?"

"We prayed and thought about the readings from the Bible. And we talked about the things we could do."

"Like what?" I asked.

"Come with me some time and see for yourself," she said.

I didn't think so. I hated boring grown-up meetings.

Chapter Fifteen

I thought it would be great to have Saint Sebastian on my detecting team. After all, he had bird dog blood in him and I was hunting a bird. Unfortunately, Saint Sebastian had a hard time focusing on just one bird.

Every time I took him out for a walk, he pointed at woodpeckers and pigeons and even a hawk. But so far, he wasn't pointing at anything that looked like an owl. "There's one! There's another one! And look over there, there's another one," he seemed to say, pointing this way and that. It was like when my little cousin learned how to say "no" and he kept saying it over and over again until everybody wished he would just stop talking. Saint Sebastian kept pointing at bird after bird, like he thought he was so smart. It was very annoying.

Saint Sebastian wasn't as good a listener as Senator Something, either. That was important when you were trying to put clues together. You needed to say them out loud to see how they sounded. It helped when you could say them to your detecting partner. Senator Something would always howl with a question mark when he thought I was following the wrong trail.

Saint Sebastian was too busy showing off what a brilliant bird dog he was to listen to me. Like he was waiting for someone to give him a gold medal or something. I wish he'd just find Chickcharney.

I complained about him to Senator Something. He just looked at me as if to say, "I told you so. Wasting your time with a bird-brained mutt who thinks he's a detective."

"Don't be mean, Senator Something," I said.

I called the zoo again. I left another message. No one called me back. My hunt for Monica's bird was going nowhere.

And no one seemed to care. No one seemed interested in the bird. Except me. And Monica. The president stopped tweeting about the State of the Union bird. Instead, he tweeted about immigration. He tweeted about Papa, too, saying some mean things.

"All part of the job," said Papa, as we walked home from the Capitol together. But he pressed his lips together and shook his head when he read the tweets on his phone.

"I'll never be a politician," I mumbled.

Papa looked up from his phone. "Why not, mija?"

"I wouldn't like it if people said mean things about me. And I don't like meetings where people talk and talk and talk."

"I have to agree with you there," he said. "But it's the nature of the beast. Politics is all about talking and talking. What else don't you like?"

I thought about it for a minute. I liked it when people clapped for Papa at his campaign rallies. I liked the balloons that fell from the ceiling on election night. And I really liked the building where Papa worked, the U.S. Capitol. But then I remembered more things I wouldn't like to do if I was a politician.

"I definitely don't want to call people up on the phone and ask them for money for my election. And I'd be embarrassed to knock on the doors of strangers to ask them to vote for me. Sometimes I don't know why anyone wants to be a politician, Papa."

"It's the way you change the world," he said. "One way at least."

I sighed.

"You don't have to be a congresswoman to make a difference, you know," he said. "You'll find a way."

Gabby was practically dancing around the living room when we got home.

"Tonight, Papa? You promised," she said.

Papa didn't say anything, but he opened the drawer in the media cabinet and pulled out Gabby's smartphone. He held it up in the air. "No more belly piercing?" he asked.

"Nope. I'm thinking about getting a tattoo instead."

"Gabby!"

"Just kidding, Papa. I promise."

Papa sighed and handed her the phone.

"Yes!"

"Dinner in five minutes!" shouted Abuelita from the kitchen.

Papa looked at his watch and ran upstairs to change out of his suit. Gabby ignored me and the rest of the world as she started checking her texts.

"Did it hurt?" I asked. "The piercing in your belly."

She looked up. "Honestly? It hurt like crazy."

I hoped I wouldn't do stupid things, like getting my belly button pierced, when I was a teenager.

Sitting alone in my room after dinner, I couldn't stop thinking about the case. I knew I should have been doing math. But Michael at school told me that there was a bird camera for Burrowing Owls out in California, set up by the San Diego Zoo.

There were actually two cameras. One showed the midget owls standing around on the dirt or peeking out from behind big rocks. The other one focused on the nesting area. That video was in black and white, which made the owls look scary. Their gigantic eyes stared at the camera and made you feel like they were watching you, figuring out whether you'd be as tasty as that cricket in the corner. Or maybe watching you to see if you were the person who was supposed to hear their message.

The website said Burrowing Owls were in danger of going locally extinct so the zoo made fake burrows where they could build nests. Those zoo burrows looked like the concrete boxes the electric company uses for underground meters.

I watched the birds for a long time. Usually, owls hung out in trees. These guys seemed happier close to the ground. Or even under the ground.

Underground! If Burrowing Owls liked to hang around underground, maybe everybody was looking for the bird that pooped on the president in the wrong place. Instead of looking up, they should have been looking down.

That meant the basement, the place where Monica worked.

Chapter Sixteen

On Wednesday, after walking both of my dogs, I stopped by the Carry Out. Monica was a blonde today.

"I have an idea," I told her. "I'm going to look for places that a Burrowing Owl might hide out."

She nodded her head and the yellow braids swung back and forth. "I feel he is somewhere nearby," she said. "And he's been eating the plate of hamburger bits I leave out for him."

I still wondered whether it was the bird or the mice in the Capitol who finished off Monica's plate of leftovers every night.

From the Carry Out, I walked along the skinny hallways of the old part of the Capitol. I ran my fingers along the walls of painted brick. No cracks were big enough to hide a nine inch bird with long legs. But here in the basement hallways of the older part of the Capitol, it was the opposite of fancy. There were no chandeliers, no statues, no pictures painted on the ceiling. In fact, you couldn't even see the low ceiling because it was covered with naked pipes and bundles of wires. It felt owlish.

I walked past the elevators, over to the other side of the basement, where the Republican members had their weekly lunch. Maybe there were scraps of chips and crusts left around for a hungry owl to finish off.

Nope. The cleaning people had cleared up everything. They'd probably also cleaned up Monica's snacks for Chickcharney.

Next, I headed over to the long underground hallway that sloped down from the Capitol to the House office buildings. If you were going to the Rayburn House Office Building, you got to ride in a little subway car that looked like a carnival ride. If you were going to the Longworth or Cannon House Office Building, you had to walk.

The wide floor was concrete. One long wall was covered with paintings by high school students from every state, from Alabama at one end to Wyoming at the other. I saw the pictures every time I walked this way. Until today, I never looked at the wall on the other side of the hallway. It was like somebody forgot to hide the guts of the building. Two white pipes, fat enough for Senator Something to fit inside, ran along the long wall. They were pretty ugly. That must be why they had put all the high school art on the opposite side. Nobody noticed the pipes because you were too busy looking at the paintings.

I watched staffers and Capitol police officers and tourists and lawmakers as they walked down that hallway. Not one of them looked at the wall with the pipes. Most of them were looking at their phones.

I thought about my first case, the mystery of the Demon Cat of Capitol Hill. One time, I had to find a disguise that would let me blend in with a group of eighth graders on a tour of the U.S. Capitol. I had decided that the best disguise was no disguise at all. And it worked. Nobody noticed me.

Maybe that was what the Burrowing Owl was doing: hanging out in this busy hallway, hidden in plain sight among the pipes on a wall that nobody noticed. Everybody who had been looking for the bird that pooped on the president was looking up. I was looking down. Maybe it was a good thing that I was so short.

I started at one end of the hall and slowly walked toward the other end. I took the flashlight out of my backpack and turned it on. I pointed the light into the dark corners. Nothing.

I kept walking.

Wait. What was that? Tucked underneath the pipes, I saw a pair of enormous eyes. They were nearly all black, with a slim rim of yellow around the edges. They stared at me, as if to say, "What do you want?"

The bird was coated with thick, fluffy feathers, splotched with brown, black, and white. He turned his head to the right to get a better look at me. And then he turned his head upside down. He bobbed his head up and down and then scooped it from left to right, as if he was keeping time with music only he could hear.

Then he stood up. For an owl, he was a small-ish, roundish bird. But when he stretched out his long, long legs, he became twice as tall.

"Chickcharney! I mean, Burrowing Owl! I've been looking all over for you!"

The bird looked a bit startled.

"Shh, it's okay. It's only me. I'm a detective and I've come to help you deliver your message to Monica. It is for Monica, isn't it?"

The bird turned its head upside down again, but said nothing.

"You can trust me," I said. "I'm Monica's friend."

Still he said nothing.

"Or maybe…you have a message for me?"

He blinked. Twice. But didn't open his beak.

"I've got to get Monica!" I said and dashed out the door to the Carry Out.

Monica had a line of customers. Her head was bent over her Bite machine. I guess it wasn't working again.

"Monica, Monica!" I said. "I found him. Chick-charney!"

Monica looked up.

"Wait your turn, kiddo," said a staffer standing in line.

"But ..."

Monica gave me a warning, signaling with her eyes. I followed her glance and saw Mr. Banks, Monica's boss, standing with his arms crossed over his chest. He was watching Monica and frowning.

Monica continued to fiddle with the machine.

I backed out of the Carry Out and thought about what to do next. I needed someone to help me catch the bird. I needed a Capitol policeman.

If there was one thing you could always find in the U.S. Capitol, it was a policeman. They were at every entrance, standing next to the metal detectors. They guarded the offices of the Majority Leader and the Minority Leader and a bunch of other big shots. They kept an eye on the tourists in Statuary Hall and the Rotunda. And almost always, they marched two by two down every hallway of the Capitol.

Except tonight. I couldn't find a single person in uniform in any basement hallway. Was everybody taking a break at the same time?

Then I remembered the underground entrance, near the Cannon House Office Building. Staffers used it when they took special guests on a private tour. There were two metal detectors and a lot of police there. Even at night. That entrance was at the other end of the hallway, past the high school paintings.

I peeked to make sure the owl was still there. He glared back at me with his yellow eyes, like little lemon moons.

"Be right back! Don't move." I told him and walked really fast down the hallway. I didn't want to get yelled at for running.

There were four officers. Unfortunately, one of them was the mean one who yelled at me all the time when I forgot to show my family pass. Or when I forgot not to run inside the Capitol. She was the same policewoman who yelled at Senator Something the time he jumped up on the table with the model of the National Mall and bit off the Washington Monument.

"You again," she said.

"Excuse me," I said as politely as I could manage. "I found the bird."

"What bird?"

"The one that pooped on the president."

All the police turned around.

"You found the eagle?" she asked.

"He's not an eagle. He's a Chickcharney. I mean, an owl. A Burrowing Owl."

"Right."

"Come see for yourself if you don't believe me."

"You'd better check," said one of the other policemen. "Just in case."

The policewoman sighed. "Show me," she said.

"You won't hurt him, will you?"

She rolled her eyes.

"Promise?"

"Yeah, yeah. I promise," she said.

I took her back down the hall to the spot where I found the bird and pointed.

"Well?"

I looked at the spot. The bird was gone.

"He – he was here a minute ago," I said. I started looking in and around the other pipes. Where was he?

"I don't have time for this," she said. "And you are nothing but trouble. First a Demon Cat, now a mysterious chicken …"

"Not a chicken. Chickcharney. You have to believe me. I found the bird that pooped on the president."

"I'm tired of you wasting the taxpayers' money, dragging me around Capitol Hill on a wild goose chase…"

"I told you. He's not a goose. He's an owl. Chickcharney."

"That's it. I'm calling my boss. If you're lucky, he'll just take away your family pass. Or maybe he'll kick you out of the Capitol for the rest of your life."

"But …"

She turned around and walked back to her post at the metal detector.

Could she really take away my pass? Could I really get thrown out of the Capitol for the rest of my life?

"Fina!"

It was Monica.

"You found Chickcharney?"

I pointed. "He was right there. But he's disappeared again. And I'm in trouble with that policewoman. She wants to kick me out of the Capitol!"

"Chickcharney," said Monica. "So close. Did he tell you his message?"

I shook my head. Now Monica would never find out what Chickcharney had to tell her about her restaurant. And I would never know if the bird had a special message for me. Instead, I could lose my family pass and never be allowed back into the Capitol. I'd never be able to find that bird.

Chapter Seventeen

Gabby had band practice on Tuesday night and Papa had a meeting. Abuelita said she wasn't going to let me stay home all by myself and told me to put on my coat "right now."

"Where are we going?" I asked.

"You'll see."

I saw that it was Our Lady of Refuge. You could hear the meeting even before you walked downstairs to the hall. I smelled coffee, which usually meant cookies, too. If nothing else, I'd get dessert by hanging around with Abuelita.

"Fina!" Three people cheered as Abuelita walked through the door. This time, I knew they were calling to my grandmother.

"And you brought an extra pair of hands!"

I guess that meant me. I half waved.

"This is my granddaughter Josefina," said Abuelita. I hated it when she used my full name. "She's very good at making posters."

I really wasn't very good at making posters, but Abuelita pushed me over toward a table in the back where a bunch of ladies and some teenagers were sketching out letters on big pieces of orange and yellow cardboard. "We have a dream, too," said one of the signs. "Immigration reform now!" said another.

"They're for the march next week," said one of the boys. He looked older than Gabby with long, curly hair and smiley eyes. "We're going to walk from the White House to the U.S. Capitol to demand immigration reform. Want to make one?" He pointed to the stack of blank poster boards.

"I guess," I said.

He handed me a black marker and a blank sign. "Here. Write whatever you want. In English or Spanish. Or draw a picture."

"What should I say?" I asked.

"What do you want to say?"

I thought about that. What did I want to say? I was grateful that Abuelita was able to be a real citizen, voting on election day for Papa, and even serving on a jury one time. Abuelita said it was the second happiest day of her life when she raised her hand and swore to "support and defend the Constitution and laws of the United States of America." Her first happiest day was the one when she married my Abuelito.

I didn't know how to put that into words, so I drew a flag with stripes and stars and a woman standing in front of it with her hand over her heart. She looked like Abuelita. Kind of. I put some glitter on the flag and used the black marker to write the words, "My American Dream."

While we were making posters, Abuelita was sitting with a bunch of people in the front of the room near the stage. They were all mumbling until a man with wild gray hair waved a stack of note cards in the air.

"Now, there's a good chance some of us will be arrested," he said. "I want you to put your name on one of these cards, and the name of the person you want to come bail you out of jail. And be sure to write down their cellphone number."

Jail! Was Abuelita going to go to jail?

"And remember," he continued, "don't resist. Just let yourself go limp. That will slow them down and they'll have to pick you up to arrest you."

"They'll pull a muscle if they try to pick me up," shouted one man who was as round as Father Andrew was tall. Everyone in the room laughed. Nobody seemed worried about going to jail. Nobody except me.

Someone started singing.

> "We have waited, waited forever
> But hope is in the air
> A new day is coming
> Lord, hear our prayer."

More people joined in. Pretty soon everybody in the hall was singing the song, holding hands, and rocking back and forth. It was as if the more they sang, the braver they became.

> *"Our days were lived in shadow*
> *But sun is breaking though*
> *A new day is coming*
> *That's meant for me and you."*

I could feel my skin tingle. These people, even my own grandmother, were willing to go to jail to deliver their message.

Their message. I remembered that bird myth on the Audubon website, the one that said when a bird flies into a house, you should expect an important message. Maybe Chickcharney's message wasn't for Monica or the president or even for me. Maybe the message was for Congress.

Chickcharney was an immigrant to Washington. Maybe he came from California, like me. Maybe he came from Mexico, like Abuelita. Maybe his message was for Congress to stop fighting and start voting to fix immigration.

I heard a familiar voice singing badly and loudly. It was Father Andrew. He asked everyone to join hands for a prayer. People bowed their heads. They prayed that their march would change hearts and minds. They prayed for the kids they called the Dreamers, the soldiers and college students who were brought to this country as babies and grew up as Americans, even though people called them illegals. Kids who couldn't even remember the country where they were born. The group prayed for lawmakers and the police. And then everybody said "amen" and there was a big rush for the dessert table.

There was coffee and a few juice boxes and lots of cookies. I grabbed a grape juice box and a handful of chocolate chip cookies, but Abuelita gave me the evil eye and I put two back.

On the walk home she asked, "Well? What do you think?"

"Are you really going to get arrested, Abuelita?"

"Maybe," she said. "But probably not."

"What would Papa say?" I asked. "Won't he be mad?"

She was quiet for a minute. "Arturo is my son and he will love me no matter what. But yes, he might be angry. Sometimes, mija, you have to do things that make other people mad if you want to change something that is wrong."

Chapter Eighteen

After school the next day, Senator Something almost pulled my arm off, dragging me over to the west side of the Capitol to the giant concrete wading pool where he liked to slurp the water. "Except it's not summer, Senator Something, and they take the water out in winter, remember?"

That orange dog is as stubborn as any U.S. Senator. He wanted to go see for himself.

It was usually pretty quiet on this side of the Capitol because the tourists didn't like hiking up the hill to get to the Visitor Center. But this afternoon, there were dozens of people, all of them marching up that hill. And Senator Something wanted to go say hello to every one of them.

"Sit, Senator Something," I told him. He sat, but he wasn't very happy.

The marchers carried signs. They were the signs we made in the church hall. Even my sign! I could tell because I'd outlined the stars in glitter glue.

"America was founded by immigrants," read one sign. "The Statue of Liberty weeps." "Immigration reform now!"

They sang some of the songs from the church meeting. Someone tooted a trumpet and someone else banged a drum. A group of nuns marched, and so did some moms pushing their little kids in strollers. I recognized the boy with the smiley eyes who helped me make a protest sign. Then I saw someone else I recognized: Abuelita.

I looked around to see if the police were on their way to arrest her. Nope. No police. At least not yet.

She waved to me. I waved back.

"Come, join us, mijita," she shouted.

I wasn't sure whether Senator Something and I should join the protest. If the police took me to jail, would they arrest Senator Something, too? What would Congresswoman Mitchell say if her dog was behind bars? Senator Something woofed, as if to say he spent a lot of time behind bars – or at least, behind the wire cage of his travel crate. "It's not the same thing," I told him. "In jail, you don't get doggie treats."

Abuelita waved again. Maybe I should join her. But then I thought how hard it would be to hold a protest sign and a leash at the same time.

While I was deciding, a bunch of reporters and TV camera people pushed past us. Senator Something barked. One of the reporters turned around. It was the one with the salami, Vicki. "Hey there, Senator Something," she said. "Sorry, no time for lunch today."

She hurried off to catch up with the other reporters. Senator Something wanted to follow her, but then I saw a bunch of police headed towards the protestors. Some of the police were on horses. Senator Something growled. He didn't like horses.

"Let's get you back to the office," I told him.

"Fina! Come quick!" Gabby called. "It's Abuelita. On the news!"

I ran downstairs just in time to see some of the marchers, including one of the nuns, lay down on the marble floor under the rotunda in the Cannon House Office Building. None of them was Abuelita.

"Six people were arrested," said the news lady, "including a member of a religious order and three college students."

"So where's ...? There she is!" said Gabby.

There she was. Abuelita was being interviewed by the TV reporter.

"Why are you marching?" asked the reporter.

"We march for justicia, for justice," she said. "We march so that America can embrace all of the people who work to make this a strong country."

The reporter looked like she was done talking to Abuelita and turned to talk to another marcher. But Abuelita wasn't done talking to her.

"We march for people like me, who came to this country many years ago to make a better life. And look at our familia now! My son, he is a U.S. Congressman."

That made the reporter interested. "And who is your son?" she asked.

"Congressman Arturo Mendoza."

Gabby and I looked at each other. Was Papa watching the news tonight?

When Abuelita got home, she went right into the kitchen. We wanted to ask her about the TV news, but she had on her "don't talk to me" face. Gabby tried anyway. "What's for dinner, Abuelita?"

"Menudo," she said.

The soup took a lot of work because you had to clean out the intestines from a cow. It sounded gross, but it tasted pretty good. It was the soup you gave people who had a headache after drinking too much the night before. I think Abuelita knew Papa was going to have a different kind of headache tonight.

When Papa got home, his ears were red. I noticed that people in Washington who don't wear hats or earmuffs in winter get pink ears. But Papa was wearing the wool hat that he called a fedora. It looked like a hat from an old black and white movie. I figured his ears weren't red from the cold. They were red because he was mad.

"Where's your grandmother?" he asked instead of saying hello.

"Buenas noches, Arturo," said Abuelita, walking out of the kitchen with a wooden spoon. "Taste."

"I'm not hungry," he said. He hung his heavy coat on the stand near the front door. The fedora went on top. He peeled off his gloves and stuck them into the coat pocket and untied his scarf and stuck it inside one of the coat sleeves. People did that in D.C. so they wouldn't lose their scarf. I never lost my scarf because I never wore one.

"Is something wrong, Arturo?" asked Abuelita.

"You know exactly what's wrong, Mama. How could you?"

"I was just —"

"The Minority Leader read me the riot act. Called it a 'stunt.' Said I was grandstanding, using my own mother to pressure the Gang of Eight. Or the Gang of Five, as it is now since a Democrat has dropped out," said Papa.

"I was just exercising my First Amendment rights, mijo," she said. "My freedom of speech."

"Your First Amendment exercise embarrassed me in front of my colleagues. And if that was your goal Mama, you succeeded."

"But mijo —"

"I'm going upstairs to change, Mama."

"But dinner –"

"I ate at the Capitol. I'm going to make a few phone calls and see if I can undo the damage. Good NIGHT, Mama."

Gabby and I looked at each other. Papa was mad. Really mad.

I always thought things would be better once Abuelita got here. I thought Papa would come home for Abuelita's dinners and Gabby would be less crabby and our Washington house would smell more like our house back in L.A. I was wrong.

Things weren't better. They were worse.

Chapter Nineteen

When I got home from school the next day, I found Abuelita stuffing her suitcase with everything in her closet.

"What are you doing? Where are you going?"

"Not now, mija," she said.

She put her shoes in paper sacks and her underwear in one of those zipper bonus bags you get when you buy makeup.

"Are you going on the casino bus to Baltimore?" I asked.

"Fina, you can help me by letting me think. Vete!"

Go away! Was Abuelita really leaving us? Was she going on a little vacation? Or was she moving back to Los Angeles?

I tapped on Gabby's door. "Can I come in?" I whispered.

"I'm busy," she said.

I tried the doorknob. It was locked.

"Gabby, it's important. Open the door. Please!"

I heard her sigh a Gabby-sized sigh, but she unlocked the door. She threw herself on her bed. "What do you want?"

"It's Abuelita. She's leaving."

"What do you mean she's leaving?"

"She's packing everything, her toothbrush, that ugly garden angel statue, even the graduation picture of Mama. She's going away, Gabby. And I don't think she's coming back."

"She can't do that," said Gabby. "Who'd take care of you?"

I didn't even fake laugh.

"What are we going to do?" I asked. "Papa is still mad at her."

I'd never seen Papa so mad before. At least not at Abuelita. Was he afraid of getting kicked out of Congress? Or at least kicked out of the Gang of Five? What would Gabby and I do without Abuelita around? Would Gabby go back to cooking burnt meatloaf for dinner?

"We've got to get them to apologize to each other," said Gabby.

"How?"

"I don't know." She picked up the pillow shaped like a giant pair of lips without looking at it, then dropped it back on her bed. "We've got to stall Abuelita. Where's her phone?"

"Plugged in and charging in the kitchen."

"Go get it," said Gabby. "Hide it."

"What difference will that make?" I asked.

"How's she going to call a rideshare if she doesn't have her cellphone?" asked Gabby. "Go. Now!"

I ran downstairs and unplugged the phone. I looked around for a good place to hide it. The silverware drawer? No. Too obvious. My room? No. That would be the first place she'd look. I ran into the living room. Now that all the moving boxes were unpacked, the bookshelves were full. Even more than full, they were overflowing.

"Fina!" shouted Gabby.

I could hear the thump, thump as Abuelita dragged her suitcase down the stairs. I had to do something. Now.

I picked the bottom shelf, full of Papa's old history books. Abuelita hated leaning over because she said it hurt her back. She'd never look at the books down there. I stuck the phone behind three fat biographies of Lyndon Johnson and rushed away from the scene of the crime to look out the window.

"I wonder when Papa is getting home," I said, trying not to sound suspicious. I really did wonder when he was coming home. He had to stop Abuelita.

"I don't know and I don't care," said Abuelita, putting on her scarf and gloves. Gabby crept down the stairs behind her. She waggled her eyebrows at me, as if to ask whether I'd hidden the phone. I nodded as Abuelita walked into the kitchen.

"Have either of you seen my cellphone?" she asked.

We didn't answer. I didn't like to lie because then I'd have to tell Father Andrew in confession.

I heard Abuelita opening and shutting kitchen cupboards and drawers. I followed Gabby upstairs. She called Papa.

"I know you said not to disturb you during your Gang of whatever meetings, Papa. But listen!" she whispered into the phone. "You have to get home. Right now! It's Abuelita. She's leaving."

I heard Abuelita coming up the stairs.

"I gotta go," she told Papa. Gabby hung up and looked around for a place to hide her own phone. Under the pillow? In her underwear drawer? She ran from spot to spot as Abuelita's footsteps got closer. Finally, she tossed it into a black leather boot in the closet. She looked around and grabbed a couple of sweaters from the closet floor. "What do you think, Fina?" she asked in a fake voice. As if Gabby had ever asked my advice about clothes. "The black one or the red one?"

Abuelita knocked, then opened the door, not even waiting for a "come in."

"Where is it, mijas?"

"Where is what, Abuelita?" Gabby asked.

"My phone. My phone. Don't play estúpido with me."

We said nothing.

"I'm very disappointed in you. Both of you."

She stomped back down the stairs.

"What now?" I asked Gabby. She shrugged her shoulders. We both crept out to the landing.

"Lucky for me," she said in a loud voice, "Your father's house is just three blocks from the subway."

"I know," I whispered. "Let's hide her coat."

It was freezing cold. Even Abuelita wouldn't be foolish enough to go outside without her red coat. I ran downstairs and grabbed it from the coat rack by the door. I turned to run back upstairs, but the coat wasn't coming with me. Abuelita had a grip on the other sleeve and wouldn't let go.

"I'm leaving, mija, and that's final." She pulled the coat out of my arms and put it on.

"Abuelita, you can't go. Who will take care of us?"

"That's up to your father now," she said.

Gabby ran downstairs. "Please, Abuelita. Just talk to Papa."

Abuelita had her suitcase in one hand and opened the door with the other. "I have nothing to say to your father."

"And why not?" It was Papa, just in time.

"Talk to her, Papa!" I told him.

"I have a subway to catch," she said.

"It can wait," said Papa, closing the front door. "Now, let's go sit down in the kitchen and talk."

Abuelita was like a cartoon character. You could almost see steam coming out of her ears. She stared at Papa. He stared right back.

"Fine," she said, pushing her suitcase into Papa's arms. She marched into the kitchen.

"You have to make her stay, Papa," I said. "You have to."

"Don't worry, mijas."

Papa took a deep breath and walked into the kitchen. He shut the door. Gabby and I looked at each other. Mama called eavesdropping a sin, punished by hearing something you wouldn't want to hear. We didn't care. Gabby and I crept closer to the kitchen door.

We didn't have to. Abuelita was as loud as a delivery truck backing up. "Say what you have to say, Arturo and be done with it."

"Mama, what is this all about? Really? It's more than our disagreement over your immigration protest."

There was a pause. Abuelita spoke in a quieter voice. "I came to Washington to be of use, to help you and the girls, the way I did in Los Angeles after Grace died. But you do not need me anymore. None of you."

"Of course we need you, Mama."

"Everything changed in those months that you were living here without me. Those girls have grown up. They make it very clear that they are embarrassed by their grandmother, that they do not need me to walk them to school or offer an opinion about the clothes they choose to wear."

"You're wrong, Mama. They do need you. I need you."

"You are too busy to need me, mijo. So I thought I would find someone who does. Those immigrants without papers, they need me."

"That's why I'm working on immigration reform, Mama. And you have to let me do my job. Talking to TV reporters makes that impossible. Do you know how upset leadership was when that TV interview aired? I got called into the Minority Leader's office like I was an eighth grader caught smoking in the boy's bathroom. Please, Mama. For my sake, for the sake of the cause you care so much about, stop. Please."

"I cannot, mijo. For once in my life, I have a chance to make my voice heard. To make a difference in this world," she said. "I will not be silenced. Not even by my own son."

Gabby and I looked at each other. Papa spoke again in a voice so soft, we could hardly hear him. "Promise me at least you'll sleep on it, Mama. Please?"

We heard a chair scrape against the kitchen floor. Gabby and I scrambled away from the door to avoid getting caught.

"Fine," we heard her say. "I will sleep on it."

Abuelita came in at bedtime to turn off my light and listen to my prayers. But I could tell that she was thinking of something else.

"Are you still mad, Abuelita?"

"Maybe I should just go back to California. I am of no use to you here."

"But who will take care of us?"

She didn't answer, just kissed me on my head and turned off the light.

Chapter Twenty

The next morning, she was gone.

"Not to worry, mijas," said Papa. "She'll be back."

But she wasn't back by the time Papa and I walked home from the Capitol that afternoon. Or by the time Gabby got home from band practice. Papa ordered pizza for dinner, but he didn't eat more than half a slice.

"Why hasn't she called me?" he asked nobody in particular.

Gabby and I looked at each other. She nodded.

"I hid her phone," I said quietly.

"You what!"

"We thought she couldn't leave if she couldn't call a rideshare," said Gabby. "I guess we were wrong. Now we can't call her or text her."

"We're sorry," I said.

Papa sighed. "Not to worry, mijas. You were using your heads, trying to keep her here."

"What are we going to do, Papa?" I asked.

Papa started calling all the relatives back in California.

"No, Arturo," said Tía Catalina. "She's not here."

"I'm going to call the police," said Papa.

"No, wait. Don't do that," said my aunt. "She's fine."

"She called you?" he asked. "Where is she?"

"Listen, Tutu," said Tía Catalina. "You know Mama. She just needs to let off some steam. Give her some time."

Papa sighed. "How much time?"

"Patience, Tutu," she said. "Patience."

Papa hung up with Tía Catalina and started looking through his emails. Then he started to frown.

"Fina, what's this all about?"

"What's what all about, Papa?"

I was at the kitchen table, looking at a map of the basement of the U.S. Capitol that I had drawn. Tomorrow I was going back to look for the bird.

"An email from the Capitol police," he said.

I think my mouth dropped open.

"It was that mean Capitol policewoman," I said. "All I did was try to show her Chickcharney. The bird that pooped on the president. But by the time she followed me over there, the bird had disappeared."

"Maybe your grandmother was right," said Papa, "letting you run around the Capitol unsupervised, treating it like your own personal playground."

"I wasn't playing, Papa. I was detecting."

"Enough, Fina. If you'd put half the effort into fractions that you put into your detective hobby—"

"It's not a hobby, Papa. Monica needs me. She needs to hear the message. I need to hear the message."

"What message?"

I didn't answer. How could I tell him that Chickcharney might have a message from Mama?

"Fina."

It got so quiet in the kitchen, I could hear the hum of the refrigerator. Was that the reason Abuelita left us? Was she mad that I was walking dogs and looking for Chickcharney instead of doing homework?

"Was it my fault, Papa? That Abuelita left us?"

Papa put down his phone. "Mijita," he said, crushing me in a hug. "Your grandmother's disappearance has nothing to do with you. She's just mad at me."

He walked around the kitchen, opening cupboards. He found the last of the sugar cookies and put them on the table. He took out two glasses and filled them both with milk. Then he sat down. He pushed one of the glasses toward me. We dunked our stale cookies and ate them, not saying a word.

When the cookies were gone, Papa brushed crumbs from his fingers.

"I remember one time when Tío Tom and I were really little and your Abuelita found out we'd been playing down by the train tracks. It was the first time I'd ever seen her get really, really angry. She yelled so much, her head practically exploded. It scared me. I didn't realize that she was scared, too. Scared that we'd get hit by a train."

"Why were you playing by the train tracks?"

"Because Tommy and I loved trains. We'd seen the old ones at Griffith Park and wanted to see a real one up close."

"I think Abuelita was right to yell at you."

Papa laughed. "I do, too."

"But she stopped being mad at you, right?"

"Eventually," he said. "And eventually, she'll stop being mad at me again."

"And eventually," I asked in a quiet voice, "Abuelita will come home?"

Papa nodded and finished his milk.

I thought about that email from the Capitol police. I felt a pain in my stomach. "Can they take away my family pass, Papa?"

"They can. You were disrupting the work of the Capitol police."

"But Papa—"

"Lucky for you, that's not what they're asking. You can keep your pass, but you have to stay out of the Capitol. At least for now. You're only allowed inside, unsupervised, for two reasons. One, if you're on your way to look for me. Or two, if you have some official business there."

"But Papa, I was there on official business. I was looking for the bird that pooped on the president."

"That is officially not your business, mija. You are to – and I quote here from the email – 'leave the bird hunting to the professionals'. Do you understand?"

"But nobody's looking for the bird anymore except me and..."

"Fina."

"Yes, Papa. I understand."

But I also understood that Monica needed my help. I had to find that bird.

Chapter Twenty One

Ms. Greenwood asked me to stay after school. That was never a good thing. I waited until everyone had left the classroom. Becka smiled in a mean way as she walked past me. Michael mouthed "good luck" before he left the room. Then it was quiet. I slowly walked up to her desk.

"It's about your math, Fina," she said. "You seem to be falling behind."

"I turned in my homework."

"Yes, you did," she said. "But there were a lot of mistakes."

I don't know why, but I hiccupped a cry. I never cry. Or hardly ever. It was embarrassing.

"I don't understand why I'm so stupid in math," I said. "When I was in kindergarten, I could add up to twenty one faster than anyone in my class."

"Twenty one?"

"My Abuelita taught me blackjack as soon as I could hold the cards without dropping them."

"Ah," she said. "But fractions are different."

Ms. Greenwood dragged a chair next to her desk and nodded at me to sit down.

"I hate fractions."

"They're not so bad."

"They're the worst," I said, throwing down my pencil.

Ms. Greenwood picked it up. She tapped the pencil on her knee. "Think of fractions as a puzzle," she said.

"Like a mystery?"

"Exactly!"

"I'm pretty good at mysteries," I said.

"See? That means you'll be pretty good at math, too. All we need to do is untangle the mystery bits."

I thought about how to solve mysteries. You gathered your facts, interviewed the witnesses, and started connecting the dots. How could I possibly connect the dots for fractions? Fractions were like the jigsaw puzzles Abuelita used to "noodle around with" on rainy or snowy afternoons. A big mess. She'd try a piece here or there and if it didn't fit, she'd try another piece. "I'm patient," she'd say. "Something you could try."

Maybe Abuelita was right. Maybe I needed to be patient. Maybe instead of throwing the whole box of puzzle pieces on the floor – something I only did once – I could be a little more patient with fractions. Maybe.

"You need a formula," said Ms. Greenwood. "Once you figure out the formula, you can solve the problem. Let's figure it out together," she said, taking out a clean piece of paper. She wrote out the problems from yesterday's homework, the ones I got wrong. I stared at them. They seemed like a tangled ball of yarn, impossible to find the right string to pull.

"The main thing is to treat the numerator and the denominator differently," she said. "Here, let me show you."

We worked together for about an hour. I still didn't understand all of it, but at least fractions didn't seem like an impossible tangle. I knew now to watch out for those tricky denominators that could change their identity if you weren't careful.

I looked at the clock. "Uh-oh! Senator Something will be waiting," I said.

"Everybody knows somebody important on Capitol Hill," she said, shaking her head. "I don't think I know that particular Senator. Is he from Alaska?"

"No, he's from Georgia. Except he's not a real senator. He's a dog. Congresswoman Mitchell's dog. I walk him. It's my job."

Something was up with Senator Something. He didn't wag his tail like crazy when I came to pick him up for his afternoon walk.

"Is he sick or something?" I asked Congresswoman Mitchell.

"You noticed it, too," she said. "I'm thinking about calling the vet." She scratched his head behind his ears, usually his favorite thing in the world. "I think he's tired of me spending all my time at those immigration meetings."

"The Gang of Five," I said.

She sighed. "It's likely to be a Gang of Four by Friday."

"Are you quitting, too?" I asked.

"Seems like a waste of time. Nobody can agree on anything. Democrats and Republicans barking at each other and neither side listening to anybody."

"Maybe you should take Senator Something with you," I said. "Then at least you'd have a Gang of Five and a half."

"Not a good idea," she said. "That dog is more stubborn than any member of Congress."

"Who's being stubborn?" I asked.

"The Democrats. They want to open the door to every Tom, Dick, and Harry who wants to come to this country," she said. "When does it stop?"

I heard that noise again, the one that sounded like the dentist's office.

"Argh! I wish they'd get done already," said Congresswoman Mitchell.

"Who?"

"The Architect of the Capitol. They're fixing the Rayburn garage. The concrete down there is quite literally falling apart. A piece of the ceiling even fell right on top of a car. Not my car, thank goodness. They've been working on that garage for weeks. The noise is so loud, it shakes the whole building. At least they don't start until after five."

I looked at the clock. It was only four thirty.

"Usually," she said.

Congresswoman Mitchell patted her dog on the back. "Go on, Senator Something," she said. "You'll feel better after your walk."

Senator Something didn't think so, but he let me hook the leash to his harness and followed me out the door. We crossed the street to the park over the parking garage. I let Senator Something stand around inside the empty fountain, usually one of his favorite things to do. He yawned. It was as if he was saying, "Who cares?" Was Senator Something depressed?

I tried talking to him about Abuelita. No response. I tried talking to him about the case. "So, guess what, Senator Something? I saw the bird! In the basement." He ignored me, sniffing around one of the concrete benches. "Did you hear me, Senator Something? I found Chickcharney! But by the time I got the Capitol police to come help me capture him, the bird was gone. He disappeared before I could hear his message. Then I got into trouble for taking the policewoman away from her job and now they won't let me back into the Capitol!"

Senator Something finally looked at me. His mouth drooped. I could tell he felt bad for everything that had happened. He gave a little sad howl. He agreed with me that the policewoman was just being mean.

"But I'm not going to stop my investigation."

His ears snapped to attention in surprise.

"I just have to stay out of the Capitol," I said. "For a while, anyway. There's still questions I need to answer and I can look for answers without setting foot inside the building. For example, how did that bird get into the Capitol in the first place?"

Senator Something wasn't listening. He was looking at the bare branches of the trees in the park. I looked up, squinting into the setting sun to see what he was looking at. "It's just a pigeon, Senator Something," I said. "And what do you care about birds? You're not a bird dog."

That seemed to make him mad. He looked at me and grumbled.

The gray bird flew off. It circled the trash cans for a while. Senator Something barked at the pigeon, as if to say, "I can be a bird dog if I want to be a bird dog."

The pigeon didn't care. It snatched up half a French fry and flew across the street. It disappeared into the archway of the loading dock of the Long-worth building.

The loading dock! That's how the bird got into the Capitol! If Chickcharney flew into the loading dock, he could fly down the basement hallway all the way to the underground entrance to the Capitol! It would be a long way for a bird to travel, but a bird could fly right over the heads of the Capitol police who stood near the metal detector.

"What do you think, Senator Something? Is that how Chickcharney got into the building?"

He thought about it a minute. One of his furry eyebrows went up, a look that seemed to say, "maybe."

"I've got to test my formula."

Senator Something gave a little whimper. He didn't seem to think that was such a great idea.

"I know, I could get into real trouble if I got caught inside the Capitol. But Monica needs me. And nobody else seems to care. Abuelita said sometimes you have to do something that makes other people mad if you want to change something that is wrong. Ignoring Monica's bird is wrong. I've got to do something to help her."

I didn't add, "And help me, too."

The orange pooch thought about that. Then he barked. He agreed!

"Now," I said. "I just need to find an official reason to be inside the Capitol again."

I didn't tell Senator Something, but that reason was Saint Sebastian. I was a dog walker and one of my dogs belonged to the House Chaplain, and the House Chaplain had an office in the basement of the U.S. Capitol. So I had to go back inside. I had to go to the basement.

The next afternoon, I tried to look normal as I walked toward the Capitol entrance, but my hands were sweaty inside my gloves. What would happen to me if they figured out I wasn't allowed inside? Would they call Papa? Throw me into the Capitol jail? Was there a jail in the Capitol?

Turned out, I didn't need to worry. Nobody paid any attention to me at all. There wasn't a wanted poster with my picture on it. My name wasn't on any sort of list. The Capitol police at the entrance barely glanced at my family pass as I walked through the metal detector. But if Papa found out, that would be another story.

First, I poked my head into the Carry Out. Monica wasn't working at the cash register. Maybe she was on a break.

Next, I headed down the steep staircase to the House Chaplain's office. Saint Sebastian was happy to see me. He seemed to smile, his tongue hanging out the side of his mouth.

"Ready to go, Saint Sebastian?"

"Is that you, Fina?" came a voice from the other room.

"Hello, Father Andrew."

"He's been waiting for you all afternoon. How's the weather outside?"

Father Andrew didn't have a window in the basement. He didn't know it was a bright, sunny day.

"It's cold," I said, leaving out the sunny part. "How about I take Saint Sebastian outside to do his business and then we'll do our laps inside where it's warm?"

"You're the expert," said the priest.

So that was what we did. I cleaned up after the little dog and put the baggie in the trash can. As we walked back inside the Capitol, I told Saint Sebastian about my investigation.

"I actually saw Chickcharney," I said. "I think he's really an owl with super long legs. But by the time I told Monica and got back to the pipes, he was gone. I need you to use your bird hunting skills to find him again. Do you think you can do that?"

Saint Sebastian wagged his tail like a windshield wiper. I figured that meant "yes."

"First, we're going to see if I'm right about how the bird got into the Capitol in the first place. We'll retrace his steps. Or actually, his flight path."

We started at the loading dock for the Longworth House Office Building. We followed the underground hallways that led from the House office buildings to the U.S. Capitol. When we got to the metal detector I again flashed my pass, and we walked into the hallway with the pipes and the high school art. I looked up. The ceilings were really high. High enough for an owl to fly over the heads of a bunch of bored police officers.

We walked over to the Carry Out. Still no Monica. Then we walked around the old part of the Capitol basement, looking for signs of the bird. The little dog sniffed the ground while I looked up at the wires and pipes overhead. Nothing.

We searched around the huge pipes in the hallway with the high school art. Saint Sebastian was more interested in the little trash cans than he was in finding Chickcharney. And then he had to go to the bathroom again.

"You may be a bird dog, Saint Sebastian, but you're not much of a detective."

It was getting late. My investigation would have to wait until tomorrow.

Father Andrew met us at his office door. "You two were gone a long time." The tall priest had a pair of reading glasses propped up on his bald head. I never saw him wear glasses at mass, or even at the immigration meeting in the church hall.

The immigration meeting! Of course. I bet Fr. Andrew knew where Abuelita was hiding. He could tell me if she was okay. But priests have to keep secrets when people tell them things in confession. Could he tell me the truth about Abuelita? Had she asked him to keep her hiding place secret?

I scratched the top of Saint Sebastian's head to take up some more time while I thought about how to get an answer. Just ask, I told myself.

"Father Andrew, have you seen my grand-mother?"

Father Andrew paused. "I see her all the time at the immigration meetings. And at church on Sundays."

That was not what I was asking, and I thought Father Andrew knew it wasn't what I was asking. I had to make it clear to him how important it was to get a real answer.

"We're all worried about her. She and Papa got into a terrible fight and then she disappeared. She didn't tell us where she was going. She didn't even take her phone. Do you have any idea how to find her?"

Father Andrew looked down at the blue car-pet. I could tell he was trying to figure out how to answer me. Finally, he looked up.

"Fina, your grandmother is safe and sound. I promise you'll hear from her soon."

Soon. How soon?

Chapter Twenty Two

Abuelita was gone for three days. We kept waiting for news. Nothing. Every day, Papa called Tía Catalina.

"She's perfectly all right, Tutu," she said. "Stop worrying."

But Papa kept worrying. "Where could she go? She has no friends," said Papa. "I really should call the police."

Father Andrew had promised we'd hear from her soon. When would "soon" get here?

I decided that we'd waited long enough. "Call Father Andrew," I said.

"I need more than a prayer."

"He might know where she is," I said.

"Why would the House Chaplain know where your grandmother is hiding?"

"Because I saw him at one of her meetings."

"Meetings?"

"Her immigration meetings," I said. "Abuelita made lots of new friends at those meetings. They even call her Fina. I bet she's staying with one of the other ladies who marched with her on Capitol Hill. And I bet Fr. Andrew knows which one."

Papa stared at me for half a minute and then kissed me on the forehead.

"I'm beginning to think you really are a detective," he said.

I was right. Abuelita was staying with a lady from the immigration march. Father Andrew gave Papa the phone number. The only problem was that Abuelita wasn't ready to come home.

"Here, you talk some sense into her," said Papa, handing me the phone.

"Abuelita? Are you okay?"

"Right as rain," she said, using one of her weird expressions. How is rain right or wrong?

"When are you coming home?" I asked.

"Home to California?"

"Home to Capitol Hill," I said. "We need you," I added.

"Apparently you do not," she said. "You and Gabby and even your father are embarrassed to have me around."

"Not embarrassed. Exactly..." I said.

I hated talking over the phone. It was always so much better when you could talk to a person face to face. I wished that I could talk to Abuelita in person. But how? Then I remembered her Tuesday night immigration meetings at Our Lady of Refuge. Today was Tuesday.

"Are you going to the meeting tonight?" I asked.

"Por supuesto. Of course. Your father cannot stop me," she said.

"I think he knows that, Abuelita. He misses you, you know."

"A fine way he has of showing it."

"It wasn't Papa who got those people arrested at the protest."

"He could have stopped it," she said.

I sighed. I would have to talk to her in person. I had to talk Papa into letting me go to tonight's immigration meeting.

Papa said the only way I was going was if he took me himself. So both of us walked down South Capitol Street to Our Lady of Refuge. Papa sighed a lot as we walked.

"What is it, Papa? Are you worried that Abuelita will yell at you again?"

"Seems like everybody's yelling at me these days," he said. "Another congressman has dropped out. We're now the Gang of Four."

"Why don't you quit that Gang of Four?" I asked.

"That would be like giving up," he said. "Mendozas never give up."

I thought about that. Maybe that was why I couldn't give up detecting. I had to help Monica. I couldn't quit.

Maybe that was why Abuelita was acting so stubborn. "Papa," I said. "Abuelita is a Mendoza, too."

Papa nodded his head.

Papa opened the heavy door to the meeting room under the church. The warm air blew around us. There were cardboard boxes near the front of the stage. Cans of corn, tomatoes, beans, and soup were stacked up high on all of the folding tables. There were tubs of oatmeal and little jars of baby food and fat packs of diapers.

Kids about Gabby's age and ladies older than Papa were packing boxes and bags with food. I didn't see Abuelita.

The room was full of ranchera music. Some people were singing along.

"Congressman! Welcome!" Father Andrew stuck a stack of brown grocery bags under his arm and held out his right hand. "Come to help out?"

Papa shook the priest's hand, looking confused. "I thought this was the immigration meeting."

"It is," said Father Andrew. "But tonight, we're packing food boxes for some of our parishioners. You know, the ones without papers and the ones without jobs."

"Right," said Papa. "I was hoping to see my mother."

"Tutu!" said a voice coming from the kitchen. "I'm in here."

Of course she was. Abuelita wasn't happy unless she was in a kitchen. It was like her laboratory, the place where she cooked up secret formulas to fix everybody's problems.

We pushed open the door and found her stirring a giant pot of something on the stove. It smelled like albondigas soup.

"How are you going to pack soup?" I asked.

"And I'm happy to see you, too!" she said, wagging a finger at me. Then she opened her arms for a hug. It felt good to be squeezed in her arms, to smell her sunscreen and soupy smell.

"Hungry?" she asked. "The soup is for the volunteers, not for the food boxes. If you feed people, it makes them happy." She gave Papa a dirty look. "Most people, anyway. And happy people work even harder."

"Are you ready to come home, Mama?" he asked.

"I am ready to serve some soup. Here, make yourself useful," she said, throwing a towel to Papa.

He caught the towel, sighed, and tucked it into his belt like an apron. Sometimes Papa remembered that Abuelita was still his mother and she could still order him around like he was a little boy.

"Soup bowls?" he asked.

"Over in that cupboard," she said. "Fina, you can get out the spoons and napkins," pointing to drawers on the other side of the sink.

Papa held out a bowl in each hand and Abuelita carefully scooped out some soup. She didn't spill a drop. She didn't spill when she filled the other bowl, either.

"Where do you want them?" he asked.

"On the empty table in the hall."

Papa took bowls of soup, two at a time, out to the hungry volunteers. Abuelita winked at me, a wink that said she wasn't really mad at Papa anymore.

"Go on," she said. "Take out the spoons and napkins."

I smiled and hurried out, passing Papa as he was coming back for more soup bowls. Somehow, Papa and Abuelita would work it out. Maybe someday all those angry people in the Gang of Four would find a way to work it out. Maybe all they needed was some of Abuelita's albondigas soup.

Chapter Twenty Three

Abuelita didn't come home with us that night. Or the next day. On Friday afternoon, Gabby and I were upstairs when we heard the key in the front door. We thought it was Papa. It wasn't.

"Is somebody going to come help an old lady with her luggage?"

It was Abuelita. Gabby and I practically tripped over each other as we ran down the stairs and into her arms.

"Are you really back, Abuelita?" asked Gabby.

"Back for good, Abuelita?" I added.

"Good or bad, I'm here."

But what would Papa say when he got home? Would they start fighting again? Would somebody say, "I told you so" and make the other person mad? Would Abuelita pack up her things and leave again?

It seemed like forever until Papa got home. I waited near the front door, peeking out the window every five minutes. Finally, there he was! I opened the door before he could even get his key in the lock.

"Are you the official greeting party?" he asked. Then he sniffed. Abuelita had spent the afternoon in the kitchen, banging pots and pans and forbidding Gabby and me from going in to see what she was cooking. Whatever it was, it made Papa smile. He started to walk toward the kitchen.

"Wait, Papa!" I said. I didn't want Abuelita to yell at him for interrupting. I didn't want them to start fighting again. I didn't want Abuelita to leave.

"I think you should stay out of the kitchen," I whispered. "You know how it is when Abuelita is the Cooking Queen.

He laughed and patted me on the head, heading upstairs to change out of his work clothes. I even heard him whistle.

Abuelita set the table like it was a fancy dinner party. She used the good dishes and even folded the paper napkins to look like little swans.

Gabby and I kept looking at Abuelita, then at Papa, and then at each other. What if one of them said something wrong, something that would make the other one mad, something that would lead to another fight that would end with Abuelita leaving for good.

Abuelita and Papa were polite, talking about how the 14th Street Bridge construction was slowing down traffic, how Tío Tom was going to have to get glasses, how it was almost starting to feel like spring in Washington, D.C.

"That was a fine meal, Mama," said Papa, kissing her on the forehead. "Thank you."

"De nada, mijo," she said.

Papa went upstairs. Abuelita smiled and watched him go. Then she looked at us and frowned.

"If you two have nothing else to do but stare at me, you can make yourselves useful by taking the dirty dishes to the kitchen. I'm going to take a nice, long bath."

Saint Sebastian wasn't at the Capitol on Friday. Father Andrew was on a retreat and took his dog with him. So the only dog I had to walk was Senator Something. Again, he kind of ignored me.

"What is with you, Senator Something?" I asked.

He just stood there, waiting for me to hook up his leash, like I was his servant or something.

"The love affair is over," said John the staffer. John thought he was so funny. He wasn't.

"Looks like he's mad at you," said Congresswoman Mitchell.

"Mad at me!"

I thought about it. Why would Senator Something be mad at me? What did I do? I hadn't even seen him since the last time I took him for a walk with St. Sebastian. Wait a minute. Could it be? St. Sebastian? Was Senator Something jealous of another dog? Of course! He was acting just like Gabby when she thought Abuelita was paying more attention to me than to her. That was it! He was jealous of me and Saint Sebastian!

I knelt down beside him.

"You're a pretty silly dog, Senator Something," I said.

He stiffened up and looked in the other direction. I whispered in his ear. "You know you're my number one pooch. Always."

He turned around and looked at me through a tangle of orange fur.

"Always," I said.

Senator Something howled.

"You're right. You're right. I did try to hunt that bird with Saint Sebastian. But that's because he's a bird dog and I thought he could help find the Burrowing Owl."

He laid down on the carpet and covered his ears with his paws. He didn't want to hear any more.

"No, you're right. You're a pretty good bird dog, too. You spotted that pigeon that flew into the loading dock. And that was a very important clue."

I knelt down next to him and scratched his ears. "Just because I worked on this case with Saint Sebastian doesn't mean that I don't love you. I need you, Senator Something. You're the best dog detective I know!"

He tilted his head and looked at me to see if I was telling the truth.

"We're detecting partners, you and me. You're good at sniffing out clues and I'm good at putting the puzzle pieces together. We're a perfect team."

He put his head in my lap and sighed. He was heavy, but I didn't care.

"Saint Sebastian is just an assistant. To both of us," I added. "You're my number one."

He wagged his tail, thumping it on the carpet.

"Okay, partner?"

He jumped up on all four feet and barked.

"I think he forgives you," said Congresswoman Mitchell.

"I think you're right," I said.

"Dogs," grumbled John the staffer.

"Claudia, what happens when you hit a dead end?"

She looked up from the files on her desk. "What do you mean?"

It was Saturday, but I still came to Capitol Hill with Papa. He had to work. Gabby was practicing her clarinet, playing the same stupid song over and over and over again. I couldn't think and I needed to think about my investigation. I took my case book with me to look at my notes.

Papa had a meeting with his Gang. He had talked a senator into coming back to the group to help work on an immigration bill. It was now a Gang of Five again.

And if Papa was working, so was Claudia, his "number one staffer." Claudia always had to remind him that she was his Legislative Assistant, not a staffer.

"What dead end?" she asked.

"When someone doesn't return your phone calls, what do you do?"

"Well, if you're a congressperson, and a witness refuses to come testify, you can send a court order. It's called a subpoena."

"But what if you're not a member of Congress?"

"Hmm," she said. "You wanna tell me what this is all about?"

I plopped down on the couch across from the front desk. I told her about Monica and Chickcharney and the Burrowing Owl. I didn't tell her about any secret message, but I told her about the zoo and how they weren't returning my phone calls.

"You know how they deliver those subpoenas?" she asked. "They knock on the door."

She picked up her car keys and glanced at the clock on the wall. "It's lunch time. Want to get a hot dog at the National Zoo? And as long as we're there, we could just go knock on the door at that bird house."

Chapter Twenty Four

It was March, but it didn't feel like spring would ever come to Washington. As we walked around the Zoo, we only saw a few families, most of them heading back to their nice, warm cars. A few ladies pushed strollers around the animal cages, their babies bundled up with so many sweaters and blankets, you could hardly see their faces.

Claudia studied the zoo map and pointed. "The bird house is that way."

There were fences and scaffolding and workers wearing hardhats and yellow vests over puffy jackets. The skeleton of a new building was there, but it didn't look like there was any place for a bird expert to work.

"Hmm," said Claudia. "Let's ask at the main office."

Just as we turned to go, a lady in a hardhat walked toward us. A badge was clipped to her vest. On it was a picture of a bird.

"Excuse me," I said.

She stopped and turned around.

"Are you the bird lady?"

She smiled. "I guess you could say that. I'm an assistant curator for birds."

"Are you missing an owl? A Burrowing Owl?"

She looked around, as if she was worried that somebody had heard my question. Then she squatted down next to me. "You don't look like a reporter."

"I'm not," I said. "I'm a detective. And I'm investigating the case of a bird that might be the one that pooped on the president."

"How do you know it's an owl?" she asked.

"I've seen him. He looks exactly like a Burrowing Owl. Is he one of yours?"

"Oh, sweetie," she said. "The owls have been gone for months."

"Did they escape?"

"No, nothing like that. We decided to reorganize our bird exhibit. The Burrowing Owls didn't quite fit in with what we had in mind."

"But I saw them on your website."

"I guess nobody's updated it yet."

"Did you let the owls go free?"

"No, of course not. We found them a new home. With the Burrowing Owl sanctuary in Southern California. The owls are back home, safe and happy," she said.

"Oh." I was glad the birds from the National Zoo were safe and happy. But what about Monica's Chickcharney? Was he safe? Was he happy?

"Those little fellows really made themselves at home here at the Zoo," she said. "They didn't mind the visitors looking at them all day. They didn't even mind the traffic over on Connecticut Avenue. Of course they wouldn't. Burrowing Owls aren't bothered at all by carbon dioxide. I'm just sorry you missed seeing them."

"Me, too," I said.

I had hit another dead end. My brilliant solution wasn't so brilliant after all. But if Monica's bird didn't come from the Zoo, it had to come from somewhere.

"Is there any place else in Washington where you could find a Burrowing Owl?" I asked.

"Not unless somebody smuggled one over the border," she said. "People get caught smuggling exotic birds all the time. Particularly drug dealers for some reason."

"Really?" asked Claudia. "I can understand people smuggling fancy parrots and cockatoos, but an owl?"

"Burrowing Owls are pretty hard to resist," said the bird lady. "They're cute and have a lot of personality. They're the kind of bird you'd just love to tuck into your lunch pail and take home with you."

Claudia and I looked at each other. Maybe someone had tucked Chickcharney into their lunch pail and brought him back to D.C.

A bunch of construction workers were walking toward us, probably coming back from lunch. The bird lady glanced at them, frowned, and then stood up. "Sorry, I've got to go," she said. "Another meeting."

Everyone in Washington had another meeting.

"Ready to go, Fina?" asked Claudia. "Or do you want to see the pandas?"

"Hah, hah," I said. Claudia knew that I thought pandas were boring. All they ever did was eat leaves and poop.

On the drive back to Capitol Hill, I wrote down in my case book all the things the bird lady had said about owl smuggling. Was she telling the truth when she said that all of the zoo's owls had been safely packed up and shipped to California? If so, why did she keep looking around, as if she was afraid someone would hear her talking about the owls? Could a drug dealer have smuggled a Burrowing Owl into Washington? Did it escape when the drug smuggler was busted by the police? And what was it that the bird lady had said about carbon something?

"Penny for your thoughts," said Claudia.

"I don't want a penny," I said.

"I mean, what are you thinking about? You've been pretty quiet."

"Claudia, what's carbon diox ...?"

"Carbon dioxide? It's a chemical. Co2. A greenhouse gas. One of the things that makes smog."

"So it comes from cars?"

"Mostly. Not my car, though. Remember, it's electric."

When we got back to Capitol Hill, we had to wait a couple of minutes before turning into the underground parking garage. A man held up a "stop" sign while a big truck backed into the Rayburn garage, its cement mixer spinning round and round.

"I hope they finish the construction soon," said Claudia.

Finally, the truck disappeared and Claudia pulled into her parking space. Papa didn't have a car, so I didn't go into the Rayburn garage very often. And when I did, I always got lost. There were doors along the walls, but I could never remember which one went to which hallway. And it was dark. It was the perfect place for a bad guy to hang out.

A bad guy or an owl. Could Monica's Chick-charney be hiding out here? And if so, how could I find him?

"C'mon, Fina," said Claudia. Your dad will be wondering what happened to us. No, this way.

They've blocked off that part of the garage for the construction."

I followed Claudia, looking in all the dark corners for a pair of eyes like lemon moons.

Chapter Twenty Five

Papa was still working at his desk when Claudia and I got back to the office.

I flopped down on the couch and flipped through my case book, looking over my notes. I was pretty sure the bird got into the Capitol through the loading dock. And now I had a clue about where he might be hiding.

But if I did find him, then what?

I opened Claudia's laptop and researched how to catch an owl. One website said you could sometimes trick them by playing sounds of a similar bird. Other experts said that food was the best way to get an owl's attention.

To actually catch the bird, you spread a net between the branches of a tree. When it got caught in the net, you dropped a towel over its head to calm it down, and then you carefully grabbed the bird with gloved hands.

That sounded scary. And all of the websites said to leave owl catching to the experts. Owls had strong beaks and sharp claws. You didn't want to mess around with wild animals. The internet said that D.C. Animal Care and Control was the place to call if you found a wild animal in trouble. I wrote down their number. I still didn't have my own cell-phone. I'd have to borrow one in case I spotted the owl.

But what if Animal Care and Control couldn't get there in time? What if it was up to me?

Papa stuck his head in the door. "Turkey wrap and iced tea, please," he said.

Papa said to go over to the Capitol Carry Out. "Food in the vending machines has probably been there since Bush was president."

"Won't I get in trouble for going into the Capitol?" I asked.

"Not if you go straight there and straight back," he said.

Monica was working on Saturday, too. And she wasn't wearing a wig. She tried to smile when she saw me, but it didn't quite reach her eyes. In fact, her eyes were red.

It didn't take a detective to figure out that Monica had been crying.

"What's wrong, Monica?" I asked. "Have you seen that bird again?"

"No," she said. "It's not the bird. This is my last day working in the Carry Out."

"Are they moving you to the frozen yogurt place in the Hart building?" I loved the million and one toppings you could pile on top of the frozen yogurt from the Senate office building snack bar.

"No," she said. "I have been let go. Fired."

"Fired! For what?"

"My boss Mr. Banks found out that I was leaving food out for Chickcharney. He said that I was attracting insects and rodents."

But Monica wasn't the only one who left food bits out. There were always donut crumbs on the carpet outside of the Democratic Caucus meeting room. And you could see a trail of Fritos in the hallway near where the Republicans had their weekly lunch meeting. Why blame Monica?

"It's not fair," I said, handing Monica a stack of paper napkins to wipe her eyes.

"We were so close to having enough money to open our restaurant. Now..."

"It's my fault, Monica. I'm the one who scared off Chickcharney. If only you had been able to talk to him, to hear his message..."

"It is not your fault, my dear. Chickcharney does what Chickcharney wants to do. Do not worry about me. I will find another job. And someday, I don't know when, but someday, you and your Papa will come to our little restaurant and I will serve you pigeon peas and rice."

She tried to smile. I tried to smile back. I collected Papa's turkey wrap and can of tea and turned around at the doorway one last time. Monica's whole body seemed to sag with sadness.

There must be something I could do.

When Papa and I got home that night from the Capitol, something weird was going on. Gabby was sitting at the dining room table. With Abuelita! They were reading a big piece of paper, the directions for a sewing project. Gabby and Abuelita were sewing. Together.

"So now I sew the front piece to the back piece at the shoulders, right?" asked Gabby.

"That's right, mija. And then you sew the sides together."

Papa smiled and winked at me. "What are two of my favorite girls doing? Plotting the revolution?"

"Hah, hah," said Gabby. "Since you won't raise my allowance so I can buy some decent clothes, Abuelita is teaching me how to make my own. Instead of upcycling my old stuff."

Abuelita had made my First Communion dress and all of our Halloween costumes. Seeing her at the sewing machine was a familiar sight. What was weird was Abuelita teaching Gabby how to sew. And neither of them was yelling.

"Check it out, Fina." Gabby held up some cut out pieces of shiny black fabric. It didn't look like much.

"What is it?" I asked.

"A dress. Duh."

"Why black?" I asked. "Why not something pink or purple with flowers on it?"

Gabby made a face.

"Not exactly your sister's style," said Abuelita.

"C'mon, Fina-Finay," said Papa. "Let's see if there's any chocolate pudding left in the fridge."

When Abuelita came in to say good night, I asked her about the sewing project with Gabby.

"How did you know what kind of dress Gabby would like?"

"I did my research," she said, pointing to her phone. "Instapost."

She held up the screen. Almost all of the clothes Gabby had posted on Instagram were shiny and black.

"You'd make a pretty good detective, Abuelita," I said.

Abuelita laughed. "Where do you think you get it from?"

Chapter Twenty Six

It was time to act. I had to find that bird.

On Sunday afternoon, I started to collect every-thing I needed. I didn't have a net, but we always saved the string bags that held the tangerines. Gab-by had cut them apart for me and sewed three of them together. She didn't even ask any questions.

"Don't you want to know what I need it for?"

"Whatever," she said.

I put the orange net in my backpack and added a pair of Papa's gloves and the dish towel with a burn on the corner.

I got a little plastic bag for my bait: a dead mouse. I knew that there were lots of mice in the Capitol. And that every night, the janitors would put out yellow sticky tape traps in just about every office. My favorite janitor Carl said he'd save me a dead mouse. I felt bad for the mouse, but I felt worse for Monica.

I also borrowed a spool of thick thread from Abuelita's sewing box. I knew that owls were the kind of birds that liked to catch their dinner for themselves. I'd watched the ones on the Burrowing Owl Cam gobble up the crickets that crawled down the concrete walls of their burrow. I needed that dead mouse to do a little dancing.

We didn't have an animal cage, but I thought a pillowcase would be a good place to keep a small owl. I also packed Senator Something's favorite squeaky toy. He'd need a reward for helping me catch the bird.

I thought about bringing both dogs. But I wasn't sure that I could trust Saint Sebastian to behave himself. It was up to Senator Something and me.

After school on Monday, I borrowed the family phone from Papa's briefcase, so that I could call animal control when I found the bird. Then, I stopped by Congresswoman Mitchell's office to pick up my partner.

"Ready, Senator Something?" I whispered in his ear as I clipped on his leash.

He barked. He wanted to help. He liked Monica, too. Or maybe he just liked her hamburgery smell. But he was ready for action. We were both ready to confront Chickcharney.

I didn't have any proof that the bird was hiding in the parking garage. But it was certainly a place with carbon dioxide. I wasn't allowed inside the Capitol, but nobody said anything about the parking garage.

Senator Something stopped outside the C Street entrance. He wasn't sure he wanted to go inside. Last year, John the staffer had been driving too fast pulling out of this garage and had hit Senator Something, breaking his leg.

"It's okay, Senator Something," I told him. "We'll steer clear of the cars."

I flashed my family pass at the Capitol policeman at the entrance. He nodded. We walked inside, passing row after row of parked cars, and a whole flight of bicycles locked to the bike stands. Senator Something sniffed around some orange construction cones and an oil puddle on the concrete floor. Nothing. We walked along the walls from one side of the garage to the other. Still nothing.

"Where would you hide out if you were an owl?" I asked Senator Something.

He thought about it for a minute and pulled me over to an area blocked off by plywood walls and the kind of yellow tape you see in crime scenes on TV.

"No, Senator Something. That's the construction zone."

He didn't care. When Senator Something made up his mind about something, you pretty much had to go along with it. He was stubborn. He was also usually right.

The construction guys weren't supposed to start working until five p.m., when most people on Capitol Hill headed home. I was surprised when a giant metal door rolled up and a man drove a fork-lift into the construction zone. He didn't close the door.

Senator Something pulled on the leash.

"No. We're not supposed to be in there," I told him.

He looked at me, as if to say, "Do you want to find the bird or not?"

"Okay, okay. But be careful. And be quiet!"

Unlike Saint Sebastian, I knew that this particular dog could follow instructions.

We peeked inside the construction zone. Part of the garage's concrete floor was torn up and there was orange mesh fencing around some of the support columns.

"I still don't think it's safe, Senator Something."

He stopped. Sniffed. His floppy ears moved up and down like a horse on a merry-go-round.

"Do you hear something?"

We both paused, listening.

"Screech."

I looked at Senator Something. He nodded. It was Chickcharney, the Burrowing Owl.

There was a yellow hardhat resting on the handle of a wheelbarrow near the roll up door. I put it on. It almost covered my eyes. Almost. I tried to find one for Senator Something, but I figured he wouldn't wear it. We both started looking for clues. Nothing. Nothing.

Finally, there, near a pile of broken concrete chunks twice as tall as me, I spotted little black pellets the size of jelly beans. Bird poop. I looked up, down, all around. And then I saw them, hidden among the concrete rubble: a pair of lemon moon eyes.

Chapter Twenty Seven

"It's him, Senator Something!" I whispered. "It's Chickcharney, the Burrowing Owl."

My hand was shaking as I took the cellphone out of my backpack. I punched in the number for animal control. Nothing happened. The phone was dead. I looked at it. Papa probably forgot to charge it last night. I had no phone, no way to call in the professionals. I didn't want the bird to escape again. If I was going to catch him, I had to do it myself.

First, I had to distract the bird.

I crouched down and whispered in Senator Something's ear. "Okay. Now, I need you to stay right here and stare at that bird. Don't bark. Don't make a sound. Just let him know that you can see him and he can see you. Can you do that, Senator Something?"

He nodded. He looked pretty proud of himself. Like he could hardly wait to tell Saint Sebastian that he was the better bird dog.

I patted him on the head and unpacked my tools. I put on my gloves and reached again into my backpack. I took out the tangerine net. I tossed the kitchen towel over one shoulder and the pillow case over the other one.

My janitor friend Carl had put a dead mouse in the plastic sandwich bag. I felt the lump inside the bag and tried not to think about it.

"Sorry, little fellow," I whispered.

I found the spool of thread at the bottom of the backpack, broke off a piece, and tied the thread around the little mouse. It was hard to tie a knot with gloves on my hands, but eventually I did it. I tugged on the string a few times. The mouse jumped around. That's when Senator Something's tail started wagging.

"No, Senator Something. This isn't play time for you. This is serious detective work."

I took a deep breath. I was ready.

I could feel the eyes of the bird watching me. I picked up the mouse by its tail and tossed it a few feet in front of the concrete cave. I started tugging on the thread. The mouse jumped around. I could see the bird turn his head almost all the way around, looking at me, looking at Senator Something, then looking at the mouse. It was as if he was deciding whether he'd be able to eat lunch and escape before a little girl or a big orange dog could catch him. He hesitated. There was a flush of wings and a flash of long legs. I could see the sharp claws. The owl flew out of his concrete hiding place, grabbed the mouse, and started to fly away.

He stopped in mid-air, flapping his wings over and over again. I had wrapped the other end of the thread around and around my glove. The owl pulled the string tight. It looked like I was flying a kite. The owl was frustrated, but refused to let go of his lunch.

I only had one chance. I tossed the tangerine net at the owl. It landed right over his head and wings. That made the bird mad. He shook his body to throw it off, but the netting slipped off his back and got caught in his claws. He flapped down to the concrete floor and tried to pull off the netting with his beak. That beak looked really sharp. I wished I could call the animal control people. Too late now.

I took the towel off my shoulder and gently dropped it over the bird. He was not happy.

"Screech! Screech!"

I took another breath. I had to get the owl into the pillow case without hurting either one of us. But how could I grab the owl and open the pillow-case at the same time? Even Senator Something couldn't help me.

That was when I saw the big, empty red bucket next to a toolbox. I grabbed it, quickly turned it upside down, and dropped it right over the bird.

"Screech!"

"We got him, Senator Something!"

He barked.

And then a human voice barked at us.

"Hey, what are you two doing over there?"

I thought it was that Capitol policewoman. It wasn't. It was a lady in a hardhat and a lime green vest.

"Shh!" I said to the construction lady.

The woman clomped over in her heavy work boots. She put her hands on her hips, looking at me, Senator Something, and the bucket turned upside down.

"This is a construction zone!"

"I'm wearing a hardhat," I told her.

"But your dog isn't."

"Screech!"

"What the heck is that?"

"It's Chickcharney. The bird that pooped on the president," I said.

"You caught the eagle?"

"He's not an eagle. He's an owl. A Burrowing Owl. And he's kind of scared."

"Screech!"

The construction lady unclipped the walkie talkie from her belt. "Bert, we've got a situation here on G-1."

It was then that I realized that I hadn't had the chance to talk to the bird, to ask him if he had a message for Monica. Or for me.

There were lots of walkie talkie calls. It was now after five o'clock and half the construction crew came over to see what was going on. Then the Capitol police showed up. Finally, someone called the people at animal control.

The bird was very quiet. I knew he was afraid of all the noise and all the people and even me and the big orange dog. Finally, a man from animal control arrived with a big bird cage. He wore goggles and heavy gloves.

"All right everyone," he said. "Back away. Back away."

We all backed up and watched. The man took out a much larger net and spread it out over himself and the bucket. He crouched down and gently reached underneath and grabbed the owl's long legs. He pulled the little bird out and carefully placed him inside the cage.

I leaned over and stared at the bird. I was right. He wasn't a mythical Chickcharney with scary hands and a lizard tail. He was a little owl with spotted feathers and lemon moon eyes. A Burrowing Owl.

"That's right, little fellow," said the man. "You're going to be just fine."

The bird didn't seem to think so. He looked scared with all these people around him.

"Poor little bird." I said. The owl looked at me, those golden eyes trying to figure me out. I smiled. "Don't worry, little owl. We'll find a safe burrow for you." And then I whispered, "Is there something you want to tell me?"

But the bird was silent. The animal rescue man covered the cage and gently carried the owl to his truck. I followed him, hoping maybe, just maybe, the bird would deliver his message. The man put the cage in a little cupboard on the side of his truck and shut the door. That was that.

"Will you please call me and tell me how he is doing?" I asked.

The man nodded. The truck drove away. The construction lady growled at me to stay out of the construction zone. I nodded. Why would I come back? Chickcharney the Burrowing Owl was gone. I even never heard his message.

Senator Something and I walked back to the park across the street. It was over. Senator Something looked sad. He was a little less sad when I pulled out his favorite squeaky toy.

"Your reward for being such a good detective," I said.

I still had questions. Where did the Burrowing Owl come from? How did he end up in the Capitol in the first place? Was I right about the owl flying through the tunnel in the Capitol to get to the Rayburn parking garage? If so, how did he get into the construction area?

At least the construction lady answered the last one. "Unless this bird figured out a way to turn a doorknob," she said, "I suspect he got here through one of the exhaust shafts. Poor bird. All he wanted was a nice quiet place to hang out, away from people, and then all of us show up with our jackhammers."

We never did find out where that bird came from. Had someone smuggled him over the border in their suitcase? Stuffed him in their pocket? Was there a drug dealer out there looking for his pet owl? And why bring him to D.C.? Or was he really a magical Chickcharney, here from Monica's island of Andros to deliver a message. A message neither one of us would hear.

There was a story in *The Washington Post* about the bird. The man who usually writes about squirrels wrote about the Burrowing Owl, retelling the story of the bird pooping on the president, his capture by an animal control officer, how he was a long way from home, and inviting anyone with clues about where he came from to come forward. Nobody did. I was kind of sad and kind of happy that the article didn't mention me. I remembered how mad Papa got when Abuelita showed up on the news. I was glad I never told Papa about my investigation. Or about the message I hoped to hear from Mama.

I called Monica and told her that I'd found her Chickcharney, but he had no message.

"That's not true, Fina," she said. "Messages arrive in mysterious ways. You wait and see."

I told her I'd wait. But inside, I wasn't too hopeful.

The good news was that the owl was finally going home. The bird got to fly in an airplane out to California where he could live with other Burrowing Owls in the sanctuary run by the San Diego Zoo. I liked the idea that a California bird had come to D.C. just like me. But unlike me, he was going back to California.

Before they took him to the airport, Claudia brought me to say goodbye. The owl was going to fly down in the cargo hold. He looked scared and lonesome in his cage. His white eyebrows over those yellow eyes seemed to bob up and down as if to say, "What's going to happen next?"

I leaned in closer to the cage. "It's okay," I told him. "You're safe now." I looked around. Claudia was talking to the rescue people. I whispered, "It's our last chance, Chickcharney. Do you have a message for Monica? Or me?"

He just blinked. And blinked again. I sighed. Maybe he wasn't a Chickcharney after all. Maybe he was just a bird. "Don't worry, little fellow," I said. "You're going home. Home to California. Say hello to it for me, won't you?"

"Screech!"

Chapter Twenty Eight

Thursday night was Papa's fundraiser. Abuelita made me wear that scratchy dress again, the one she made me wear the night of the State of the Union speech. This time, though, she wasn't going with us.

"I am going to lay low," she said. "Your Papa's job tonight is to raise as much money as possible. I do not want to be a distraction."

Abuelita was a little bit famous. Reporters kept calling to talk to the protester who was the mother of the congressman working on the immigration bill. Abuelita kept telling them, "No comment."

Papa and Abuelita had come to an agreement: she could go to all the meetings or protests she wanted. She could write letters or even go on TV if she wanted to go on TV. She just had to make it clear that she was speaking for herself and not for her son, Congressman Arturo Mendoza. I think Papa and Abuelita even shook hands on it. Tonight, Abuelita was staying home. It was just Gabby and me and Papa.

"Do I have to ask people for money?" I asked Gabby as I was squeezing into those tight shoes.

"That's Papa's job," she said. "Our job is to smile and eat tacos."

Gabby was wearing the black and silver dress she had made with Abuelita. It looked pretty good if you didn't look too close at the bottom where it wasn't quite even. Gabby didn't care. She was excited to show off her new dress. Even if it didn't show off her not-pierced-anymore belly button.

Papa walked with us over to the ugly brown building of the Democratic Congressional Campaign Committee, practically right around the corner from Papa's office. He said it was close to the Capitol and the House office buildings so that lawmakers could run over during a lunch break to make calls asking for money in one of the little rooms set aside for fundraising. They didn't let you make those calls from your congressional office. It was against the rules to use a government phone or a government office to help you run for re-election.

Tonight, we walked into the big Wasserman Room. Colored lights in the corners flashed pink and yellow across the crowd and rows and rows of the paper flags called papel picados waved from the ceiling. It felt like one of my cousin's birthday parties. Except there wasn't a bounce house, and Gabby and I were the only kids in the room.

People crowded around tall, round tables with drinks in their hands. They must have been on their second or third drink because they were laughing really loud. Louder even than the trumpets of the mariachi band which was playing over on the little stage.

"There you are!"

It was Claudia. She was wearing a bright blue dress and even high heels, instead of the usual flat, boxy shoes she wore to the office. Even Papa noticed. He smiled.

"Here," she said, holding out a pink drink in each hand to Gabby and me. I tasted it. It was just punch. She handed a bottle of water to Papa. "Ready, Congressman?"

Papa patted his pocket where he'd put his speech notes. "See you later, girls. Go grab some food," he said.

There was a curry table and a Korean barbeque table and a table with little pita pockets full of spicy fillings. Gabby pointed to the sign behind the poke bowl table. "Check it out," said Gabby. "My favorite L.A. food truck! Poke Doke."

"They're all food from food trucks," said Claudia. "That was your father's idea. Since L.A. has the best food trucks in America, he thought folks in D.C. deserved the chance to try them. In exchange for a donation to his re-election campaign, of course."

"But where are their trucks?" I asked.

Claudia smiled. "It would take too long for them to drive across the country, so we just flew out the chefs and all their secret ingredients so they could cook for your Papa here tonight. And for you. Go on, find yourself some dinner. I'm going to go check the microphone setup." And she left.

"I know where I'm going," said Gabby as she headed over for a bowl of poke.

I didn't like raw fish. But I liked almost everything else. I took a deep sniff. It even smelled a little bit like California, where you could eat food from around the world without getting on a plane. But what should I eat?

One food table was really crowded. A woman was scooping up huge spoonfuls of yellow rice and nutty green pigeon peas. It was Monica.

I hurried over to the Taste of Caribbean table. I waited until the hungry crowd moved away with their food.

"Monica!"

Tonight she was wearing a curly black wig with a bright blue and gold scarf, the same colors as the flag on the wall behind her, the flag of her island country.

"Fina!" She came around the table and gave me a giant hug.

"You're here!" I said.

Monica nodded. "Thanks to your Papa, inviting me to come tonight to cook for his party."

I looked across the room at Papa. He was shaking hands with half a dozen people. But then, as if he knew we were talking about him, he looked up. I pointed to the Taste of the Caribbean table and Monica. He smiled, giving me the thumbs up.

Monica laughed. "And guess what?" She took a handful of business cards out of her apron. Everybody in Washington had a business card. It looked like Monica had collected one from everybody at the party.

"All of these people, they love my food. They want me to cook for their parties."

"Of course they do, Monica," I said. "You're the best chef on Capitol Hill."

"Shh!" she said. "Don't let the food people from California hear you! They will be jealous."

"Are you okay, Monica? Really okay?"

"I am fine, Fina. I now have the time to cook the food I love and people are paying me to cook it."

"But you never got to hear your message from Chickcharney."

"Oh, I did, Fina. It is as clear as if the bird had whispered it in my ear. Instead of a restaurant, my husband and I will buy a food truck. It is much cheaper than rent and we can take it to people's houses to cook for their weddings and parties. What do you think?"

"I think it's great. And I know the perfect name for your food truck," I said.

"Chickcharney!" we said at the same time and laughed.

"I guess Chickcharney gave you blessings after all," I said.

"Not just me, Fina. Open your eyes and see your blessings, too."

I looked around the room. My Papa was shaking hands with a movie actor from that superhero movie. Papa was the real superhero. Instead of fighting with super villains, he was fighting to fix immigration by writing a bill. Over in the corner, Gabby twirled, showing off her new dress to Claudia. Gabby could be the crabbiest person on planet Earth. But the rest of the time, I was glad she was my sister.

Then there was the blessing of Abuelita, waiting for us when we got home. And it was a home, not just a rented house on A Street SE. Abuelita left everything she had known and loved in Los Angeles to move here to take care of us in our Washington home.

Monica was right. I had many blessings. I didn't need Chickcharney to bring them to me. They were already here. That was my message from Mama.

When we got home that night, I took off my pinchy shoes and scratchy dress, and sat on my bed in my pajamas. I wasn't sleepy at all. I'd already finished my homework, including the entire math worksheet. Now that I understood the formula about treating numerators and denominators differently, it didn't take me all night to finish.

I took out my case book and wrote down everything that had happened, about finding the Burrowing Owl in the Rayburn garage and saying goodbye to him before they flew him back to California. I wrote about how the bird acted like a Chickcharney for Monica, bringing her inspiration about a food truck.

Maybe this bird, who came to Washington from someplace else, delivered a message to Congress by pooping on the president. A message about fixing immigration. I thought about all the protests and prayers from Abuelita's group and all the meetings Papa attended with his Gang of Eight. It was a Gang of Eight again. The people who dropped out of the group decided it was better to argue about something with each other than let other people argue without them. They still didn't agree on a bill, but at least they were talking to each other.

I thought about how Gabby and Abuelita still barked at each other. But not as often. And never when the sewing machine was on the dining room table.

I thought about Senator Something and Saint Sebastian. I would ask Father Andrew to say some prayers about those two. They were still acting like Democrats and Republicans, making little growling noises at each other, trying to prove who was the better dog.

I put it all down in my case book. And then I closed it and tied the piece of string around it. The case of Chickcharney was closed. The mystery of the bird that pooped on the president was solved. I was ready for my next investigation.

That was Thursday. On Friday, Abuelita was smiling when Papa and I walked in the front door. In fact, she was humming Pitbull's "I just want to celebrate" song. I started to go upstairs to dump my backpack and change out of my school uniform.

"Josefina," she said. She only used my full name when I was in trouble. I stopped on the fifth stair and held my breath.

"You have mail," she said in a sing-songy voice.

I never had mail. Except on my birthday when the tías would send cards and sometimes tuck a twenty dollar bill inside. It wasn't my birthday.

Abuelita waved a white envelope at me. What could it be? She presented it like it was a glass slipper on a pillow. My name was typed on the front. I looked to see who sent it, but there was no name in the upper left hand corner. Instead it read "The White House, Washington, D.C."

I carefully opened the envelope. Inside was a piece of paper.

> *Dear Ms. Mendoza,*
>
> *Thank you for your tireless efforts in the investigation of BirdGate. You have succeeded where the Secret Service, the Capitol police, and numerous other agencies have not.*
>
> *I understand that you have encountered resistance to your efforts to track down this bird. For that, I am sorry.*

It was a long letter.

> *Since I am Commander in Chief, I have instructed various policing agencies of the federal government to allow you to continue your important work. Please consider this letter your official permission from the president to continue your investigations wherever they take you on federal property.*
>
> *I trust that you will not abuse this privilege, but will instead use your talents to assist federal agencies whenever you are able.*

It was signed by the president! I touched the signature to make sure it wasn't just printed onto the paper. It was real. I could feel where the president's pen made a dent in the page. "What does it mean, Papa?" I asked as I handed him the letter.

Papa read it twice and handed it to Abuelita, who handed it to Gabby. Papa and Abuelita looked at each other and shook their heads.

"It means," said Gabby, "You are now officially Fina Mendoza, Girl Detective."

Did you enjoy the book? Please write a review

Please let Kitty know what you thought about *State of the Union: A Fina Mendoza Mystery* by leaving a review on Amazon, Goodreads, or your favorite bookstore's website. It will help other parents and children discover the world of Fina Mendoza.

(If you're under 13, ask a grownup to help you.)
Thank you!

Want MORE Fina?

Subscribe to
The Fina Mendoza Mysteries podcast!

Available FREE on Apple Podcasts, Spotify, or
wherever you listen to podcasts.

Sign up for the **Fina Mendoza Fan Club** and get a
free, downloadable **coloring page** of Fina and Senator Something, designed by Imelda Hinojosa.
Have a grownup sign up at our website
finamendozamysteries.com.

Acknowledgements

As always, many thanks to my friends and former colleagues on Capitol Hill, including Andy Elias from the House Radio/TV Gallery and Michael Lawrence from the Senate Radio/TV Gallery, Karen Bronson from the House Chaplain's Office, Laura Condeluci from the Architect of the Capitol's Office (who reminds me that the AOC doesn't have janitors, just "custodial positions.")

Thanks as well to members of my SCBWI critique group, Jennifer Pitts, Bohdan Porendowsky, and Debra Schmidt, my six extra eyes on this project. And thanks to Gail Eichenthal, Ronda Fox, Elizabeth Logun, and Anne Thompson, my group of scribes who root for Fina every step of the way.

Many, many thanks to the cast and crew of **The Fina Mendoza Mysteries** podcast, who brought these characters to life: Amy Solano, Monica Vigil, Steve DeVorkin, Raul Garza, Steven Cuevas, Christine Avila, Susan Valot, Linda Graves, India Sherwood, Myca Sherwood, William Beemer, Eddie Pike, Leo Schodorf, Isla Schodorf, Wenzel Jones, Laura Stegman, Elizabeth Logun, Paul Cummings, Melanie Macqueen, Steve Gamber, Rosalie Fox, Brian Bland, Mat Kaplan, Hunter Felde, and Hannah Matzecki.

Thanks to the original Fina, who solves the mysteries of first graders with a firm hand and a big heart.

And thanks to my number one fan and the best writer in the house: Tad Daley.

About the Author

Award-winning writer, public radio journalist, and TEDx speaker Kitty Felde hosts the *Book Club for Kids* podcast. With more than a million downloads, the show has been named one of the top 10 kidcasts in the world by *The Times* of London. Kitty has a remarkable talent for talking to kids and she shared her super power during her recent TEDx UCLA Talk. As a journalist, the native Angeleno created the Washington bureau for Southern California Public Radio where she reported on Congress. She's covered everything from war crimes trials to OJ Simpson to baseball, and hosted a daily talk show in Los Angeles for nearly a decade. She won the Los Angeles Radio *Journalist of the Year* award three times from the Society of Professional Journalists and the L.A. Press Club. Her many plays are performed worldwide.

Find Kitty at www.kittyfelde.com and @kittyfelde.